INDIANA.
A CLOSE ENCOUNTER.
THE THIRD KIND.

In the horror of crashing, grinding noises and flashing, blinding lights, Jillian lost track of what was happening. Barry was . . .

"Barry!"

Then she caught sight of her son. Crawling on the floor. Toward the dog door opening. He reached it and started trying to wriggle through the narrow opening.

Jillian lunged forward and grabbed for Barry's foot. She caught it and started to haul him back in. She pulled hard. He slid across the linoleum toward her.

Then something pulled him away. Some force was tugging him outside the house.

"Let go of him!" she screamed.

Jillian held on to her son until she felt that if she did not let go, he would be torn apart because the other side would not let go. Sobbing, Jillian loosened her grip and Barry slipped away from her hands and out the little door.

He was gone.

THE SPECIAL EDITION

CLOSE ENCOUNTERS

OF THE THIRD KIND

A COLUMBIA/EMI Presentation
CLOSE ENCOUNTERS OF THE THIRD KIND
A PHILLIPS Production A STEVEN SPIELBERG Film
Starring RICHARD DREYFUSS
also starring TERI GARR and MELINDA DILLON
with FRANÇOIS TRUFFAUT as Lacombe
Music by JOHN WILLIAMS
Visual Effects by DOUGLAS TRUMBULL
Director of Photography
VILMOS ZSIGMOND, A.S.C.
Produced by
JULIA PHILLIPS and MICHAEL PHILLIPS
Written and Directed by STEVEN SPIELBERG

CLOSE ENCOUNTERS OF THE THIRD KIND

The Special Edition

A Novel

Steven Spielberg

A DELL BOOK

Published by
Dell Publishing Co., Inc.
1 Dag Hammarskjold Plaza
New York, New York 10017

Dell ® TM 681510, Dell Publishing Co., Inc.

ISBN: 0-440-11332-6

Printed in the United States of America

New revised edition

First printing—August 1980

Seven misshapen figures emerged from a blinding swirl of desert sand and sage. Their images hazed in and out of tons of gushing earth. Three somewhat stupefied Federales were waiting just outside the one-horse town of Sonoyita in Northern Mexico. Honking and tugging hysterically at their hitching place, the burros sensed another intrusion and kicked at everything in sight. The figures were almost upon them now. The first building in this haunted desert junction loomed ominously. Straight up, the sun said noon, but its color was blood, matching an antique neon Coca-Cola sign within the adobe frame of some cantina oasis. The first figure out of the wind was just over six feet and greeted the three Mexican police with a curt nod and a barrage of Spanish. "Are we the first to arrive?" the khaki-clad man shouted in high school Spanish, his Rommel goggles and leather bandana hiding his nationality. "Are we first here?" he demanded.

The stunned policeman answered him by nodding southward, where another group of explorers was

materializing from thin air. And at the fringes of
Sonoyita in a desert storm in 1973 the two teams came
together, fourteen total, handshakes brief and voices
discreet.

"Is the French interpreter with you?"

The hidden face had an American voice, slightly
bucolic, maybe Ohio-Tennessee. "Yes, sir. I speak
French but I'm not an interpreter by profession." The
voice belonged to the shortest member of the second-
arriving group, and in it was the slightest suggestion
of fear. Beefing up to compete with the wind howl,
David Laughlin began to sound more important. "My
occupation is cartography, topographics. I'm a map
maker. A map maker."

"Can you speak French, sir? Can you translate
English into French, French into English?"

"If you go slow and understand this is not what
they pay me for." Interrupting, another figure came
forward and extended a hand to the cartographer and
spoke broken English with an accent that was native
French.

"You are Monsieur . . . uh . . . Low-glan?"

"Uh . . . Laughlin," Laughlin gently corrected, and
shook the hand. There was something about the
Frenchman's voice that invited soft, careful responses.

"Ah, *oui*," the Frenchman chuckled almost apologetically. "*Oui, oui, pardon.*" And then in French this
time. "And, Mr. Laughlin, how long have you been a
project member with us?"

Laughlin was proud to answer that question and he chose his words carefully.

"From the time of my country's joining with the French in '69 I attended the Montsoreau talks the week the French broke through. My congratulations, Mr. Lacombe." Lacombe smiled, but the team was itching to move on in anticipation of what they had come all this way to see. Sensing this, Lacombe led the way and began to converse with Laughlin as quickly as he went. He waved to another team member and in several seconds Robert Watts, Lacombe's personal bodyguard, was in sandy step.

"Robert, *écoute* Monsieur Laugh-o-line."

"Yes, sir."

"Say to Robert in English, Mr. Laugh-o-line, this what I say to you now, *en français. Alors.*" Lacombe rattled off a statement in French and Laughlin said it in English to Robert only a beat or so behind the spoken word.

"You are going to translate not only what I will say," Laughlin enunciated, "but also my feelings and my emotions. I must be understood perfectly."

Up ahead the Mexican Federales were shouting and pointing at things in an area being pummeled now by forty-five-mile-an-hour winds. So much dirt blew across everyone's eyes that the first object intermittently resembled a dragonfly with a fifty-foot wingspan. The men approached cautiously and the phantom shape began to tell them what had only been hearsay twenty-four hours earlier.

Something was sitting in the road, on what looked like wheels with wings, tail and propeller. There were markings on the sides and numbers on the wing. Behind it when the red wind gave pause were six others just like it. They were navy Grumman TBM Avenger torpedo bombers circa World War II.

The expedition came to a halt. Lacombe took several steps and lifted his smudged bubble goggles. There was a curious peace about him now. He seemed neither anxious nor passive as he gathered in the view. The Frenchman's face was incongruously youthful despite his gray weedy hair. Deep-cut lines started at his nostrils and ended to each side of his mouth. And as he made up his mind about what was to be done, the lines seemed to deepen. Lacombe took a breath, wiped dust from his face with the back of his hand, put on a polyethylene glove and gave Laughlin his first order to relay. Laughlin nodded quickly after the spurt of words and shouted to everyone standing there.

"I want the numbers off the engine blocks." Laughlin wondered if he hadn't made a mistake by not editorially attributing the command with the understood "he." No one seemed to care. In seconds fourteen project personnel were crawling across the wings and tail, opening hatches and unscrewing caps. Everyone wore Playtex Living Gloves. One technician rolled back the canopy. It slid open without a hitch, the grooves and ball bearings good as new. With his polyethylene glove, one of the technicians used surgical tweezers to extract a calendar stuck under the instrument panel. The calendar was a promotional item: "Trade Winds Bar, Pensacola, Florida." But the date was the best part.

"Mr. Lacombe," the gloved technician shouted breathlessly on the brink of discovery. "It's dated May!"

"*Quoi?*" Lacombe went right to Laughlin for the translation, but the technician was quicker. "May through December 1945."

Lacombe understood this only too well. He beamed and raised his voice to Laughlin. Laughlin blanched and hollered to everyone in English.

"See if there is *essence* . . . gasoline, in the tanks. See if the gasoline will support combustion."

Standing next to Laughlin was the bodyguard, his arms sagging in wonderment.

"Jesus. These babies are in perfect shape." A voice ripped the day apart in triumph. The voice sounded Southern.

"AE 3034567. Goddamn! AE 29930404. Christ! AE 335444536. Holy shit!" Laughlin left out the expletives and someone else checked the numbers against a sheet of paper.

"Numbers on the engine blocks match. So do the wing numerals." The bandana that kept the sand from Lacombe's nostrils and throat rose high around his face, his eyes were on fire as someone tested one of the Grumman's landing lights. They cut a twin pattern in the thick air.

"*C'est possible?*" Lacombe was slapping his sides,

and Laughlin, befuddled now beyond reason, nudged Robert, the bodyguard.

"Would you bring me up to date?"

Robert bent forward confidentially. "It's Flight 19."

"Go on."

"Flight 19. Don't you know? This was the squadron of aircraft departed Pensacola on training maneuvers in May '45. That was the last anyone ever saw of them. Until today. You figure it out."

"But where are the pilots? Where's the crew?" Robert didn't have the answer, he just shrugged when unintelligible hollering commenced a few feet beyond this activity. Lacombe rushed over, Laughlin on his heels. The three Federales had a collar. A tiny form huddled in the threshold of the cantina. The Mexican police wouldn't shut up, and all of their noise sounded like panic. Lacombe looked in Laughlin's direction for a little help and David had to smile.

"*Je ne parle pas espagnol. Français et anglais seulement.*"

Mr. Tennessee-Ohio spoke up. "They say this man was here. They say he was here two days. They say he saw it happen."

This was more than Lacombe or anyone had hoped for. The Frenchman dropped to one knee and with the gentlest touch cupped the humbled chin in his sterile glove. The Mexican raised his head the rest of the way. He was crying but that wasn't what riveted Lacombe. Half of the man's face was cherry red and blistered from forehead to collarbone. It was the worst sunburn Laughlin had ever seen on a leathery face so accustomed to Mexico's furnace summers. The man's hands were buzzing and a certain stench drifted up that brought Lacombe's gaze to the Mexican's starched pants. He had urinated in them some time ago and as he lifted his face to speak, he was involuntarily wetting them again. The sad, desolate man worked his lips together, forcing air through his vocal cords, trying so hard to say it. And when the words broke in Spanish, the man broke down in real tears.

"*Qu'est-ce qu'il dit?*" Lacombe breathed. Laughlin turned to the American who knew the language. But the man shrugged and questioned the humbled wreck at his feet. Again the same words croaked forward and the smell of urine was unbearable. Lacombe was a patient man but the American was keeping the words to himself for too long a time. Laughlin intervened. "What was he saying?" The American raised his eyebrows and let out a sigh along with the translation. "He said the sun came out last night. He says it sang to him."

2

Four-year-old Barry Guiler was having a restless night. A gentle Indiana breeze, floating through the half-open bedroom window, ruffled his bangs. There was a soft but persistent whirring noise coming from somewhere in Barry's room and it troubled his sleep. Suddenly a soft red glow played over his face and Barry's eyes opened.

On the night stand next to his bed, one of Barry's battered toys had somehow come on. It was a Frankenstein monster; when it raised its hands, as if to strike out, its pants fell down and it blushed.

Barry sat up in bed, staring at Frankenstein, and then looked around the room. He had a lot of battery-operated toys scattered about—a Sherman tank, a rocket ship, a police car with red dome light and siren, a model 747, a drunk hanging on to a lamppost and chugging from a bottle—and all of them were moving, flashing, whirring. All by themselves.

Barry was delighted. His phonograph came to life

all of a sudden, scratching out a tinny version of the *Sesame Street* theme song.

Barry laughed and clapped his hands. Then he jumped out of bed and ran over to the open window. Outside, in the distance, he heard a dog barking, but his back yard was dark and utterly still.

Barry's bedroom was at the end of a hallway. Very curious now, he trotted down the hall to the living room. The room was dark except for a small blue night light. Barry sensed, though, that something was different, something was out of place. All the living-room windows were wide open and the night air was breathing through the lacy curtains, stirring them in a very odd way. The front door was wide open as well, and the porch light was shining brightly against the black night.

Despite all these strange things, the little boy was not frightened. He was ready for fun. There was a funny smell coming in the open windows and door— a little like the way the air smelled after there had been a lot of thunder and lightning. But Barry didn't think a summer storm had just come through. He hadn't heard anything; he didn't hear any water dripping. Besides, this was different.

He decided to go see what was happening in the kitchen. All the windows in there were wide open, too, and the breeze was really blowing. The back door was ajar and rattling against the safety chain. But that was nothing! Bingo's dog door had got knocked off its hinges and was lying on the floor, and Bingo wasn't in his bed next to the refrigerator.

The refrigerator was open, too, and there was a lot of food—a milk carton, some Cokes, butter, a cottage-cheese container, bologna, leftover dinner—in messy piles on the floor in front of the ice box, leaving a sloppy trail all the way to the open dog door. Barry picked up a half-melted Heath Bar. Then something else in the kitchen caught Barry's attention. Several somethings. Barry spun. The Heath Bar dropped from his open hand, sliding across the linoleum. The little boy backed away so quickly he slammed shut the big Amana with his tiny body. He carefully waited, his soft eyes unmoving. And then Barry Guiler smiled—a shy playful look that seemed to invite . . . a response. Barry looked some more—and giggled and looked away—peek-a-boo—more laughter—peek-a-boo. New game. Barry looked hard; then, rocking back and forth on his heels like a chimpanzee, he spun full around, cocking his head to one side before rotating it slowly —"Like this? Like this?" He was brave. "Boo!" he shouted. And made his scariest face. "Grrrrr-boo!"— his scariest.

Jillian Guiler had been asleep in her bedroom. Jillian had had the flu all week, and her head, her bed, and the room were all in a state of general disarray. The house that Jillian and Barry lived in was small and stood by itself atop a low, rolling hill in this rural area of Indiana. It was really an easy house to take care of, but Jillian had felt pretty rotten all week and had let the housework slide.

In her bedroom, everything was everywhere but where it should have been. The same wind that had been playing through the rest of the house suddenly swept into Jillian's bedroom, picking up and dropping Kleenexes and a couple of half-finished charcoal sketches of Barry. The bedside table was a clutter of pills, nasal sprays, half a sandwich, and a can of Coke.

Jillian started coming half awake in that peculiar frame of mind that flu produces: tired but not sleepy, thinking but not very clearly, able to do something but not about to. She was under the covers but was still wearing a bathrobe. The TV set was on, and the laughter Jillian at first heard she thought was coming from the stupid sitcom that she saw flickering on the screen. But during a commercial Jillian heard the laughter again and finally recognized its source.

Barry began to imitate the thing outside, mimicking what he saw. First he covered and uncovered his eyes, as if playing peek-a-boo. Then he spun around several times like a top. He cocked his head left and right and left and right again.

He began to laugh out loud with the joy of it, moving into the night as he did so. A pale, burnt-orange light illuminated his face as he walked into the night, laughing.

It was the laughter, growing fainter, that wakened Jillian at last.

Well, that and the parade of toys. The laughter brought her half awake, wondering what had disturbed her slumber. Then, as she sat forward, eyes slowly opening, the police car came through the door of her bedroom, its dome light flashing.

Behind it rumbled the tank, fire flashing in its gun muzzle. Next the giant jumbo jet trundled forward to the accompanying whine of the police siren. And, finally, his pants dropping down, rising and falling again, Frankenstein's monster lurched in, arms outstretched.

Jillian jumped wide awake, flipped off her covers and got out of bed. The police car narrowly missed her toes as it headed for a wall and shoved its grille into the plaster. Behind it the other toys began piling up in a confused, multivehicle collision.

"Barry?" Jillian called.

Then she remembered his laughter. It had all but faded away, only the memory of it still hanging in the night air.

The bedside clock read 10:40. What in the world was Barry up to now? He'd only been in bed two hours.

Jillian staggered out of bed and went down to the hall to her son's room. Barry's bed was empty. The windows were open. She ran out of the room, back down the hall to the living room. There she stared about her wildly at the open windows, the open front door, the shining porch light.

Unmistakably now, the sound of Barry's laughter

was outside the house, out in the night somewhere.
Jillian gave a little cry and then sneezed.

The laughter again. Fainter this time.

Oh, God! Jillian thought wildly. She rushed out the
front door into the yard. Trying unsuccessfully to
adjust her eyes to the darkness beyond the porch light,
Jillian found herself whimpering. Catching hold of
herself as best she could, she cried, "Barry! Barry!"
and ran into the darkness in the general direction of
her son's disappearing laughter.

3

The world inside all air traffic control centers is unreal. There are dozens of them scattered across the United States; the one half-buried in the earth near Indianapolis is as typical as any.

The artificial world created within these great concrete bunkers is only dimly perceived. The place is dark. The only light comes from small, shaded bulbs of low wattage that barely show where the doors are.

Most of the light comes from radar screens that sweep the sky over Indiana's airspace. Here there is no day, no night, only an artificial gloom and the bright radar glowing its electronic picture of what is happening in the real world overhead.

The nation's air traffic passes in review, noted on radar, interrogated by radio, announcing itself, making proper identification, receiving approval and advice, and either landing in Indiana or, more often, passing above at speeds nearing 600 miles per hour to its destination elsewhere.

False as this dim world is, it presents what every

air traffic controller hopes is an accurate picture of real events. He hopes that every jumbo jet, every low-flying Piper Cub, is duly noted and neatly notched into an arrangement that assures everyone safe passage through the state.

That is the controller's hope. That is not what always happens.

Harry Crain was working midwatch that week. On midwatch there were only five or six men at the radar scopes. Harry usually moved behind them, pacing back and forth or resting occasionally on a tall stool, his headset connected by a long coiled wire to the radio bands in use, a small curving plastic tube that picked up his voice and conveyed it by microphone to the real world high above his head.

This night, four controllers made up the front-line team. They sat side by side, in pairs, all in open-necked white shirts, the sleeves rolled up one fold, each pair watching their scope. Above their heads, loudspeakers squawked and rasped the usual radio air traffic drone, spare now because in the airspace over Indianapolis it was as black a night as it was in the air traffic control center below.

"Air Traffic Control," a pilot's voice came in. "You have any traffic for Aireast 31?"

Harry Crain looked intently at one of the scopes. There were only three full data blocks and one partial data block. The two going in the same direction were fifteen miles apart; the third going in the other direction was a great distance away from Aireast. The rest of the scope was clean.

Harry cut his mike into the circuit. "Aireast 31, negative. Only traffic I have is a TWA L-1011 your six o'clock position, fifteen miles and an Allegheny DC-9 your twelve o'clock fifty miles. Stand by one. Let me take a look at the broadband."

Harry reached up and pushed a button. The radar scope changed from narrow band computer radar to broadband normal radar. Harry took a quick look, pushed the button again. then another button. He looked at the primary picture in computerized form. There *was* a non-beacon target in Aireast's vicinity. Harry peered at the scope more intently just as the pilot broadcast again: "Aireast 31 has traffic two o'clock three to five miles, slightly above and descending."

One of the controllers leaned over to look and grunted surprised confirmation.

"Aireast 31, roger," Harry said. "I have a primary target about that position now. We have no known high altitude traffic. Let me check with low."

Harry turned to his interphone man and said, "Call low and see if they know who this—"

"Center, Aireast 31," the pilot came back on, cutting through Harry. "Traffic's not in low. He's one o'clock now, still above me and descending."

"Can you tell aircraft type?"

The pilot's voice was matter-of-fact, considering the

information he was about to report. "Negative. No distant outline. The target is brilliant. Has the brightest anticollision lights I've ever seen—alternating white to red and the colors are striking."

The other sector controllers were now looking and listening. The coordinator reached up, pushed a button, called someone and mumbled indistinctly.

Harry sat back on his high stool for a moment and eyed the radar scopes. "TWA 517," he called to the other aircraft. "Can you confirm?"

A different voice came over the loudspeaker. "Center, this is TWA 517. Traffic now looks like extra bright landing lights. I thought Aireast had his landing lights on."

The coordinator said, "What do we have here, Harry?"

"Say again, TWA 517," Aireast asked.

The TWA pilot enunciated slowly and clearly. "Do you have your landing lights on?"

"Negative."

Harry broke in. "TWA 517, Indianapolis Center. Aireast is your twelve o'clock position, fifteen miles same direction and altitude. Ident, please." He turned to his coordinator, saying, "Aireast claims he has unusual traffic almost at his altitude. I don't know who it is."

The TWA identification appeared on the screen and Harry asked the pilot if he has the Aireast jet in sight.

"Affirmative."

"TWA 517, do you have Aireast's traffic in sight?"

"Yes," the pilot said cautiously. "We have it now and have been watching it."

"What does traffic appear to be doing?"

"Just what Aireast 31 said."

Aireast 31 cut in. "He's in a descent about fifteen hundred feet below me. Wait a second . . . Stand by one . . . Okay, Center. Aireast 31 traffic has turned and is coming right for our windshield. We're turning right and leaving flight level three fifty."

Harry Crain jumped off his stool and everyone in the dim room tensed.

The coordinator turned and said, "Get on the phone to Wright-Patterson and see what the hell they could be testing up there."

"Aireast 31, roger," Harry said at the same time. "Descend and maintain flight level three one zero . . . Allegheny DC-9, turn thirty degrees right immediately . . . traffic twelve o'clock, two zero miles, Aireast jet descending to FL-310."

The Aireast pilot, still remarkably low key, said, "Luminous traffic now in angular descent and exhibiting some nonballistic motions."

Harry and his coordinator just looked at each other and said nothing.

"Okay, Center," Aireast said conversationally. "Traffic is coming on strong. Ultra bright and really moving."

"This is TWA 517," the other pilot said. "We're going to go a little right to keep away from traffic also."

"TWA 517, roger," Harry Crain said. "Deviations to right of course approved."

"Center, Aireast 31 is out of three one zero and traffic has passed off our ten o'clock, five hundred yards and really moving."

The team supervisor, who had moved in the dim room to a point just behind Harry, spoke for the first time. "Ask them if they want to report officially."

"Aireast 31, roger," Harry said. "Report flight level three one zero. TWA 517, do you want to report a UFO?"

There was only static for several moments. Then: "Negative . . . We don't want to report."

"Aireast 31, do you wish to report a UFO?"

More static.

"Negative. We don't want to report one of those either."

"Aireast 31," Harry Crain persisted. "Do you wish to file a report of any kind?"

"I wouldn't know what kind of report to file, Center."

Harry smiled and started to relax. "Me neither," he said. "I'll try to track traffic to destination."

"And show us at level three one zero now," the pilot said, and then added, almost as an afterthought, "The stews in the back tell me that passengers were snapping pictures of traffic during that close pass."

Harry Crain turned to his team supervisor and said softly, "Those I'd like to see." Then, speaking again into the microphone, he said, "Allegheny Triple four turn right to intercept J-8. Resume normal navigation. TWA is level at three one."

The team supervisor left Harry, disappearing again into the dimness. The tension sifted out of the center.

Harry's coordinator asked, "What's in the book about this kind of thing?"

"Hell if I know," Harry Crain said. "The Air Force started writing it thirty years ago. Let them finish it."

4

Aireast 31 passed over Roy Neary's home about nine o'clock that night. Its jet engines sounded only faintly inside the house, and none of the occupants seemed to notice.

Roy had confiscated the family room of the suburban house and made it into a workroom that looked like a hobby room run by the Salvation Army. Mechanized and electrical inventions hung and lay abandoned along the walls and in the corners, and there were enough adult toys lying around to rob the children of their childhood.

The most prominent object in the room was an HO gauge railroad laid out on the family ping-pong table. The tracks ran through elaborate Tyrolean terrain, complete with mountains and lakes.

That night Roy Neary and his eight-year-old son, Brad, were alone in the room, sitting side by side. Roy was trying to help Brad with his math. Brad, a pile of arithmetic books at his feet, was considerably less interested in addition than in electric trains.

Neary had carefully explained to Ronnie, his wife, who enjoyed a game of ping-pong now and then, that a model railroad was a necessity when there were growing boys in the family.

"A necessity for the father," she had pointed out. "Like ping-pong is for the mother."

Roy had finessed the potential confrontation by promising to dismantle the railroads on weekends, but somehow, over the months, instead of being dismantled, it had grown in complexity, until it now took most of Neary's leisure time simply to keep it running.

"How about a drawbridge over that underpass?" Brad asked.

Neary frowned at his son. "I thought you were supposed to be doing your homework."

"I hate arithmetic." The eight-year-old threw down his pencil and stared challengingly at his father.

"You're not trying."

"Train engineers don't need arithmetic."

Neary picked up the pencil and put it back in the boy's hand. "Suppose," he said, "the stationmaster assigns you eighteen cars. Then he says, 'Make up two trains with the same number of cars in each.' What do you do?"

Brad threw the pencil down again and reached into his rear pocket. Out came a Texas Instruments pocket calculator. "It won't matter," the boy said. " 'Cause I'll have one of these."

Roy sighed and looked heavenward. The long moment of silence between them was fractured by Toby Neary, six years old and a tornado who carved a path of destruction into the room and yanked to a halt in front of his father. Toby was very angry. His blue eyes blazed, and he stuck a not-very-clean finger in Roy's face.

"You stole my luminous paint." Toby shouted.

"I didn't *steal* anything."

"I don't steal stuff of yours," Toby went on relentlessly.

Roy was distracted from this argument when he noticed Ronnie moving slowly into the room, eyes shut, hands out before her, groping the air like a sleepwalker.

She was, normally, a whimsical woman, with long blond hair and an oval face that came to a soft, pointed chin. Her eyes were usually wide open, often under brows raised at one of her husband's weird ideas. Now she was moving like a blind person, and a miniature replica of her seemed to be tagging along as a caboose. Three-year-old Sylvia had hold of Ronnie's long skirt and was lifting her feet up high and putting them down ever so slowly, her eyes shut tight, too.

"Ronnie," Neary started to say.

"Brad," Ronnie said, ignoring her husband, her eyes still shut, her face expressionless. "Brad, here's an arithmetic problem for you. If there are seven days in a week and your mother is home all seven of them, how many days are left to your mother?"

He didn't need the calculator. "Zero!"

"Ronnie," Neary said again. He didn't like where this was going. "Open your eyes."

"Why?" she asked. "I can walk through the whole house like this. Make the beds, put on the coffee, feed the kids. All without opening my eyes. I'm like Toby's hamster in his cage."

"No, really," Roy said. "Open your eyes. Watch this."

Ronnie's eyes opened slowly. Humming tunelessly —an indication he was pleased with himself—Neary pushed a button on the model railroad's control panel. The children and their mother watched a tiny sailboat stir into motion, gliding across a mirrorlike lake. It sailed closer to a railroad bridge, over which a train was about to roar. But as the train reached the bridge, it stopped.

The drawbridge swiveled sideways on a center pivot. With tiny tacking movements, the sailboat whirred through the open space, and the drawbridge started to swivel shut. Without waiting for it to close, the train whipped forward and catapulted neatly into space, crashing down on the lake with a metallic clatter.

Neary's grin disappeared. "Hmm."

Ronnie's stare lifted from the train crash to her husband's face. "Gee, Roy," she said in a flat tone. "That was . . . really . . . great."

"It worked a while ago."

"Um-hm." Her level stare—her eyes were an even

fiercer blue than Toby's—never lifted. "I give this railroad two more weeks," she said. "I bet it ends up in the basement with the auto-tennis and the electric toilet and all the rest."

"That's not fair."

"Okay, not all," she granted. "That worm ranch you had in here. At least you dumped that into the back yard and not down in the cellar." She picked up the newspaper and started paging through it, looking for something, anything. "Jesus, can't we do something? I'm serving time in this house."

"We got out last weekend," Neary offered.

"Walking across the street to the Taylors' is *not* getting out of the house."

"You get out every day when you take Brad to school," Neary suggested.

"It's as fully a rewarding an experience as when I take Toby to school. Or take Sylvia to the supermarket. Or take the car to get snow tires switched to regulars."

Neary winced inwardly. "You're painting a very dull picture," he said.

"Give me a different brush."

"Listen, if you think my job with the power company is some kind of glamour life . . ." Neary trailed off, wondering how angry she really was. Ronnie had the ability to burn out her anger quickly. "Listen," he told her, "when you've fixed one burned-out transformer, you fixed them all."

Ronnie stared blankly at him. "I think it's that new thing they're always talking about," she said.

"What new thing?"

"Life-style. I think we have to change ours."

"That's for rich people, honey," Roy said. "They just call up the store and order a whole new life-style."

"Maybe it isn't life-style," Ronnie said. "Maybe it's that other thing the magazines talk about . . . quality of life."

"Sounds like a soap opera."

"There has to be more to life than stalking the super-market aisles looking for three rolls of paper towels for a dollar."

Neary was silent for a long moment. She had never butted him about how much he earned, or whether they had enough money to live on. He'd always assumed they did okay.

"I got a raise in January," he began cautiously.

She shook her head. "Wrong track. I'm not talking about money. I don't mind searching for specials in the store. As long as something special is going on somewhere in my life. And, Roy," she added, "you know me. I'm easy."

"Huh?"

"I'm not asking for a week in Acapulco. I mean I'm so starved for something to happen, I'd go bananas if you brought me home a flower. One perfect rose."

Neary winced again. "I always forget that."

"When you crave change the way I do," Ronnie said, "you'll settle for anything. New potholders. Going down to the Hertz office and watching them rent Pintos. Calling time and weather and dial-a-joke."

"Listen," Toby said, intent on getting back to important things. "He took my luminous paint."

Ronnie folded the newspaper to the movie section and stuck it in front of her husband. "Play through this on your calculator," she suggested.

Neary glanced down at the page. "Hey! Guess what? *Pinocchio's* in town."

"Who?" Brad asked.

Ronnie had opened her handbag and was examining her face in a compact mirror. "I smile too much," she said. "My mouth is thinning out."

"*Pinocchio*," Neary said. "You boys have never seen *Pinocchio*. Are you guys in luck!"

Brad frowned. "You promised Goofy Golf this weekend."

For once, Toby was in agreement. "That's right. Goofy Golf."

"But *Pinocchio* is so great," Roy said.

"Thinning out," Ronnie repeated aloud to herself, "and turning mean. Just like my mother's mouth."

Brad produced a great sigh. "Who wants to see some dumb cartoon rated G for kids?"

"How old are you?" his father demanded.

"Eight."

"Wanna be nine?"

"Yes."

"We're seeing *Pinocchio* tomorrow," Neary said.

"Winning your children's hearts and minds," Ronnie commented to her reflection in the mirror.

"Just kidding," he told her. "But I grew up on

Pinocchio. Kids are still kids, Ronnie. They'll eat it up." He hummed softly for a moment, then sang a few words. "When you wish upon a star . . . makes no difference—" Neary stopped. He could see that he wasn't getting through to anybody, neither children nor wife.

"You're right," he said, throwing up his hands. "Fellas, you can make up your own minds and I won't influence you in any way. Tomorrow you can play miniature golf, which means a lot of waiting in line and pushing and shoving and maybe scoring zero . . . or . . . you can see *Pinocchio* which has music and animals and magical stuff and things you'll remember for the rest of your lives."

Then, in desperation: "Let's vote."

"Golf!" all three children shouted.

Neary pretended to stagger back. "Okay, tomorrow, golf. Tonight . . . bedtime. Right now. Get going."

"No, wait," Toby protested. "You said we could watch *The Ten Commandments* on TV."

Across the room the telephone rang. Ronnie moved to answer it. "That picture is four hours long," she said, picking up the phone on the second ring. "Hello. Oh, hi, Earl."

Neary said, almost to himself, "I told them they could watch only five of the Commandments."

"Slow up, Earl," Ronnie said into the phone. "I can't relay all that. You better tell Roy direct." She held out the phone to her husband. "Something's up."

Neary started around the ping-pong table. "My kids

don't want to see *Pinocchio*," he grumbled. "What a world."

Roy reached for the phone. Instead of handing it to him, Ronnie held it to his ear with one hand, moving around to snuggle against his other side, kissing his other ear. Neary was used to this sudden mood switch of hers. He leaned over and picked up Sylvia, who wanted to kiss his ear, too.

"What's the problem, Earl?" he asked his colleague at the power company.

"I got a call from the load dispatcher," Earl Johnson, his voice high with worry. "Big drain on the primary voltage."

"On primary?" Roy said. "How the hell—?"

"Shut up and listen," Earl cut in. "We've lost half a bank of transformers at the Gilmore substation," he said, trying to get the words out as fast as possible. "It'll hit the residentials any minute, so put on your pants while you've still got the light."

"Earl, what the—?"

"Get over to Gilmore fast, Roy."

The line went dead as Earl hung up. Neary turned toward his wife. "Did you hear that—?"

Then the room went dark. Everything stopped dead.

5

An ARP synthesizer is nothing if not complicated. There are still not many of them in the world, and still fewer people who know how to put one together, and even fewer who understand what to do with the thing: its capabilities, its potential, its limits.

Therefore, when the rush order came through to modify the synthesizer they had constructed for Stevie Wonder two years before, the bearded, mustached and bespectacled young men who understand these arcane matters proceeded with bemused diligence.

Bemused because, evidently, Mr. Wonder was lending or giving his ARP to a group not previously known for its musical interests. But what the hell? What could these guys do with an ARP synthesizer that they couldn't already do with a nuclear-tipped long-range intercontinental ballistic missile?

6

Ike Harris was holding on to two telephones when Roy arrived: one connected directly to an apartment elevator in which Supervisor Grimsby was trapped, the other to the equally-agitated outside world.

Harris was shook. "A 27-KV line at Gilmore went," he said into the phone to Grimsby; at the same time, he was briefing Neary. "All the breakers opened and we started losing feeders. Tolono's dark. Crystal Lake's dark. What? Oh, that's right, sir. You're dark too." Harris glanced at Neary and his eyes went up in his head for a moment, signaling the kind of vibes Grimsby was transmitting at his end.

"Okay, right," Ike said, when Grimsby was temporarily through screaming. "I've got reports of vandalism on the line—890-megawatt lines seem to be down all over. I called Municipal Lighting for a fix, but we can't send the new juice through till this 500-KV tower is operational. What? Yes, sir!"

Harris put his hand over the phone. "Neary, you know the normal wire tension in that area?"

"Without wind, normal tension for the sag is about fifteen thousand pounds per wire. I was a journeyman out that way a couple of years ago."

Ike took his hand away from the phone. "I'm sending Neary over there now."

"You are?" Roy mouthed.

Harris waved Neary out of the control room with the hand not holding the Grimsby-phone. "Get the hell going. On the double. No, not you, Mr. Grimsby."

As Roy started trotting out the door, he heard Ike shouting to someone, everyone, anyone: "Tell Municipal we're going to candle power in ten minutes."

Now, fifteen minutes later, barrel-assing down a dark country road whose name or number he wasn't sure about, Neary was about to admit to being lost. Roy's van was a smaller version of his workroom at home. He had a network map spread out over the steering wheel as he searched vainly for the problem coordinates, a penlight sticking out of his mouth.

Already a menace on the road, Neary was further distracted by the police calls that were squabbling over his broadband radio.

"This is Sheriff's Dispatch. Do I have a patrol car near Reva Road?"

"Hello, County. This is highway patrol six ten. We're on Reva. Can we help you boys out?"

"If you would, thank you. See the woman two eleven Reva Road. Something about the outdoor lighting. She's in a state. Barking dogs. Go figure it out."

The radio stopped talking, and Neary stopped driving, pulling over to the side of the road. Reva Road was in Tolono, he was sure of it. But Ike had reported Tolono dark. Roy picked up the mobile phone.

"TR eighty-eight eighteen to Trouble Foreman," he called.

"Here's Trouble," Ike Harris came back, no less hysterical than fifteen minutes ago. "Whaddya want?"

"Have you guys restored power to Tolono? Over."

"Are you kidding? Tolono was the first to go."

"I just heard the police reporting lights in Tolono."

"Jesus!" Harris shouted. "What, are you monitoring police calls on a night like this? Everything's down, Neary. The whole network's fallen."

Harris went off abruptly.

Neary pulled back onto the road. Several minutes later, he saw a revolving amber light in the distance, which made him feel a little better. But not much. At least he wasn't lost. Roy pulled over behind a utility trouble wagon and got out. Two crews were there, standing by, waiting for someone in authority to give the word. A yellow DWP cherry picker idled, ready to lift men to the top of the tower that loomed indistinctly high in the darkness.

Neary felt inadequate. He'd never bossed line crews before. These guys were good—old-timers, most of them. Roy had put in his time on line crews himself, but these guys were fifteen years older than he was and ten times as experienced. Just because he'd moved up through the system didn't mean a damn thing to these fellows, didn't automatically mean they'd follow his orders, if he could think of any orders to give.

Then Roy picked out a friendly face, a black one, Earl Johnson, who'd called him earlier.

"Hi, Earl," Neary said. "What's up?"

"Down," said Earl, white teeth grinning in the revolving amber light. "Why do you think somebody would steal two miles of transmission wire?"

"You're kidding."

By way of answer, Earl lifted his six-volt flashlight and aimed its beam to the top of the tower. Then he traced a line where two thick copper wires should have sagged along to the next tower. But there were no wires.

"The line's not down," he said. "It's gone. There's nothing from M-ten to M-twelve."

"I'll be damned," Neary said. "Maybe it's the high price of copper," he mused.

Earl and Roy started back to Neary's car to make their report.

"Right," Earl said. "Right. Stuff's worth a fortune. I told them we ought to lay power cable underground."

"But where could the birds land?" Neary said.

Before Roy could report to Ike Harris, the radio flashed a police call. "To any unit in the vicinity of Tolono foothills . . . a housewife reports . . . uh . . . her Tiffany lamp flashing in the kitchen window . . . upside-down lamp . . ."

"Where'd he say?" Johnson asked. "Tolono?"

"That's the second report from Tolono," Neary told him.

"Can't make it out clearly," the police dispatcher came through again. "Very distraught . . . four one five five Osborne Road."

"But Tolono's dark," Earl said.

"Maybe," Roy said, picking up the car phone. "TR eighty-eight eighteen. Let me talk to Ike." He handed Earl the map. "Find Osborne, will you?" he asked. "I never could read these damn things."

Harris came on. "Neary! What's happening?"

"Well," said Roy conversationally, "I'm here at Mary ten. And . . . all the lines have been swiped. All the way to Mary twelve, Earl here says. It looks like vandals made a very sloppy cut at the terminals, then backed a truck in and pulled out all the grounds, but here's something else—"

"Here's something for you," Ike cut in. "We've got to pick up the system in one hour."

"One hour!" Neary exclaimed. "It's a mile of empty poles out here. That's impossible."

"Anything's possible when you've got a general supervisor stuck in an elevator who wants out."

Roy gave Ike a small laugh, then asked, "Say, Ike? You haven't restored power to Tolono, have you?"

"I told you, Tolono was the first to go. It's as dark as the inside of Grimsby's elevator."

"Now look, Ike," Neary began in a careful tone. "Hear me out. The police are reporting lights in Tolono. If the lines out there are energized and it's not showing up on your data bank, one of your people working high around those terminals—*ga-zzap!* It happened in Gilroy once. Remember?"

"Me and two backup computers say Tolono's as dark as the inside of your head, Neary," Harris shouted.

Earl Johnson affected not to have heard this slur.

"See the complainants at Tolono South Reservoir," the police dispatcher suddenly called. "Christmas lights have started a minor brush fire."

"Did you hear that? They're saying Christmas lights now."

"This is May, not December," Harris said, suddenly his old cheerful self. "There is no Christmas during a blackout. Only Halloween." And he hung up before Roy could respond.

Neary turned to Earl Johnson. "What's wrong with that guy? This is how Jordie bought it, replacing shot-out insulators in Gilroy."

"You heard the man, Roy," Earl said. "He told you to fix the line."

"Right."

Neary stood there, humming softly for a moment. Then he turned back to Earl Johnson and said conspiratorially to him, "Say, Earl, how'd you like to sign on this operation for about an hour?"

He was climbing in the car, closing the door and starting the engine before Johnson began to respond.

"Me? Run this show? Who's gonna listen to me? I'm not even seniority. I'm not even white. Don't turn your back on a good thing, Roy. They made you boss cow."

"Earl, if he's wrong, some of our Tolono people could get killed."

"If he's right, they'll suspend your ass so high even the job-placement corps won't find it."

Neary started easing the car forward. "Tolono is what?" he asked out the window. "Sixty-six alternate to seventy?"

Roy drove away.

Johnson held his head in agony over Neary and his sense of direction. "You gonna wind up in Cincinnati," he yelled after him. "It's seventy to sixty-six."

Neary waved back at Johnson. Seventy to sixty-six.

A moment later, the night swallowed up the shape and sound of his vehicle.

Earl Johnson watched the taillight grow dim and then disappear. He heaved a heavy sigh and walked slowly back to the gang of linemen, watching him with a mixture of suspicion and amused malice.

Earl stood before the veteran repairmen, wondering what on earth to tell them to do. He took a deep breath and pointed toward the tower overhead. "Fix it."

Aireast Flight 31 touched down on the tarmac at 11:40 P.M. The Indianapolis tower issued routine taxiing instructions to the A.E. Concourse, a short three-minute dogleg from the east-west runway.

A brace of airport security police waited curbside, their walkie-talkies gargling squelch while a fuzzy voice told the public that the white zones were for the immediate unloading of passengers only.

A black Ford LTD carved a trail through the mild late night congestion, smoking its tires inches away from the fleet of the airport security patrol. One tire actually lurched up over the white curbside with enough noise and danger to make any cop grab for his citation pad.

Instead, one of the security officers reached for the rear door and held it open. Three men got out. Were they pro football players disguised as Sperry-Rand accounting executives? Their Brooks Brothers pinstripes looked as if they had been ironed right onto their six-foot sinewy frames. Two of the men wore sunglasses, and the other had a gray mustache that didn't quite match his short blond hair.

A fourth CPA type, nearly resembling Fran Tarkenton, came running, out of breath, through the electric terminal doors.

"It's down!"

"When?"

"Just about a minute ago. Where have you been? She's on the taxi to gate 55A."

The front four ran into the terminal annex, shouldering open the electric doors when they wouldn't move fast enough.

They charged the Up escalator, taking it two steps at a time. At the top, the first of them bounced off a woman who did not see them coming, and the other three almost piled into them. Instead, they dodged around their colleague and the woman, who was somewhat pregnant and was sprawled on the floor, and took off.

The first man picked up the pregnant lady, with many apologies, ascertained that she was all right, startled but otherwise okay, and took off after his friends. She remembered a small plastic card with his face on it, dangling from a thin metal chain around his neck.

The first man caught up with his colleagues as they trotted through the security metal detectors. They all waved their badges on their little chains at the security personnel and were waved through. Now they started sprinting down the long corridor leading to the arrival-departure gates, as if to make up for lost time.

But instead of running down to any of the gates, they suddenly skidded to a stop in front of a door marked only by a small number "6," someone remembered later, and, without knocking, charged in.

Seconds later, the front four reemerged, bringing with them three very bewildered FAA officials, wearing plastic photo IDs but having no resemblance to pro-ball players. They were angry, and getting angrier as the hastily assembled group crowded around the airport tower entrance, fumbling in pockets for a passkey.

Aireast 31, a 727, had stopped for thirty seconds, waiting out some surface traffic. Now she was moving again, heading right for the docking area 55A. Suddenly 31 hit its brakes and lurched once before stopping. The nose wheel began to shift hard to starboard.

Guiding the aircraft to the concourse was a ground attendant, his flashsticks frozen above his head. The jet continued to starboard. Anxiously, the ground attendant waved his flashsticks. "This way, over here!"

A.E. 31, totally ignoring the signal, pivoted full around and headed for a private section of runway, with blue flashing dead-end lights.

Helpless, the attendant let his sticks sag, then shrugged over toward the baggage boys, who were peering up at the control tower for signs of life.

Meanwhile, in another part of the airport—unaware of the unseemly hullabaloo taking place—Lacombe,

the proximate cause of it all, landed. His military jet
taxied off a main runway to a little-used parking area
and stopped next to a black Cadillac limousine. The
twin jet engines screamed to a stop, the door opened,
and the slight Frenchman stepped, quickly but not
hurriedly, down the metal steps, across the concrete,
and into the back seat of the Cadillac.

In the front seat of the limousine were a government driver in military dress and a man dressed in a
business suit. Lacombe, in his austere, controlled manner, waved aside all preliminaries about his trip, etc.,
and asked, "They are prepared?"

"Yes, sir," said the man in the business suit.

The driver moved the limousine farther away from
the passenger terminal to an area where freight was
stored for trans-shipment. Four other cars were already parked there, motors running, headlights off.
As the Cadillac pulled up in front of the others, a car
door opened and a young man emerged and trotted
over.

He leaned in the front window next to the driver,
and said, "Monsieur Lacombe?" It was Laughlin.

Inside Aireast 31, the wilted passengers—too tired
to complain any more and too relieved at having
landed in Indianapolis at long last—watched bleary-
eyed as the forward door was opened by a stewardess
and six large men crowded up the movable stairs that
had been pushed up to the side of the plane, through
the hatch and into the compartment. Two of the men,
in business suits, disappeared into the flight crew's

cabin while the other four—dressed in unmatching slacks, ties and jackets, their plastic badges dangling over their ties—stood by the open door and in the aisle, as though to block any exit.

By this time, all forty-four passengers had become more curious than tired, when the next thing they saw was their pilot, copilot, radio man, and flight engineer leaving the cockpit under the escort of the two men in business suits. Those passengers able to look out the starboard windows watched as their flight crew got into two waiting automobiles and were driven away. The men in suits came back up the stairs and into the plane again.

Two of the unmatching men now started moving down the aisle, handing out little pencils and small IBM cards. As they did this, one of the men in suits asked a stewardess for the cabin microphone. She gave it to him. He pushed the speaker button and said, in the false, friendly tones of a public relations man, "Folks, I'm Jack DeForest, speaking to you on behalf of Air Force Research and Development Command, apologizing for the delay in your flight and personal schedules. We really want to get you all on your way just as soon as possible.

"Okay," he went on like a shipboard social director. "This is nobody's fault, but during your flight, unknown to your pilot or Aireast Airlines, your aircraft accidentally passed through a restricted corridor where classified government testing was being conducted."

That got a reaction from the passengers: a series of grunts and muttered "I thought so's."

"Now, I said this wouldn't take long, and it won't," Jack DeForest went on. "I'm going to ask all passengers with cameras, exposed film canisters, boxes of unexposed film, and tape recording devices to turn them over to our courtesy team at this time."

Now the reaction was instant and angry. Jack held up a hand, which no one could see except the stewardess. "Just temporarily, folks. You'll have them all back within two weeks. That's a promise. You fill in those little cards we handed out with your name, address, and description of whatever you're turning over to the Air Force. And you will definitely get it all back . . . slides, prints, whatever . . . at our expense."

Jack DeForest let the complaining run its course. Behind him, Lacombe entered the aircraft, Laughlin at his shoulder. They all watched the passengers, still grumbling, begin filling in the IBM cards.

Lacombe turned sideways to Laughlin and whispered something to him in French.

"Mr. DeForest," Laughlin said, at which point the eyes of every passenger raised up to see what was going to happen now. "Tell the flight crew we need the flight recorder intact. And one thing more."

"Yes."

"Don't wash the plane."

Laughlin had snapped out Lacombe's whispered orders without thinking of anything more than translating them into English. Now, as he watched the passengers' frightened and concerned reactions, David realized it would have been smarter to have talked to the flight crew personally.

The passengers' faces reflected exactly what nobody wanted them to reflect. It had been the business of not washing the plane.

It was a bad moment. But no one spoke. Perhaps they were too tired. Perhaps they didn't really want to know. Perhaps they'd just had enough for one day.

Lacombe, Laughlin, DeForest, and the others knew that at least a couple of the passengers would start searching out the press the next day. But they felt sure that the only accounts of the experience that would ever get into print would appear in the pages of the *Enquirer,* the *Star, Argosy,* and other periodicals. Still, Lacombe, Laughlin, DeForest, and the others knew that there was no way to stop what was happening that night. It was only the beginning.

There was no way the dispatcher could get to Neary.
He'd switched off the mobile phone unit in his car.
Roy didn't want Ike Harris calling him. As he drove
through the night to Tolono, he could see a blanket
of stars above him, although the usual spring night
ground fog was rising out of the gullies, bouncing his
headlights back at him.

Neary did not ride alone. He had the police calls
for company.

"U-5. Officer Longly. Over."

"Go ahead."

"Responding to the 10-75 on Cornbread Road and
Middletown Pike. I am observing . . . I think it's street
lights in the foothill residentials. Couple hundred
neighbors in their pajamas think it's Saturday night
out here," Longly observed on the police band.

A bright group of high beams appeared over Neary's
shoulder out the back window. He was tearing at his
maps and absently waved his arm out the side window. The automobile headlights passed him, and

somebody shouted out the car, "You're in the middle of the road, jackass!"

Neary spread a map over the steering wheel, finally located Cornbread and Middletown. D-5, M-34. He took off, tires screeching.

Within five minutes, Neary was hopelessly lost. Finally, in utter desperation, he pulled into a row of darkened fast-food franchises. The blackout had, apparently, provided a perfect excuse for everyone to hang out in the parking areas. As soon as a bunch of them saw Neary's DWP truck, they crowded about him, waving flashlights and cans of Coors.

"Did your lights come back on?" he asked them.

"You asking us?" a lady in curlers and kerchief asked. "What do you do for a living?"

"What about the street lights? When they went off did they come on? On-off, on-off."

A wise-ass kid stuck a flashlight in Roy's face. "Like this?" he said, blinking the light blindingly on and off, on and off in Neary's eyes.

"Yes."

"No," the kid said, laughing cretinously.

"Am I in Tolono or where?" Neary asked Mrs. Curlers.

"It's all lit up out here," Officer Longly's radio voice said suddenly. "These street lamps . . . I think sodium vapor. Don't want to stay still. They're revolving in some draft. They go up . . . they go down . . . wait one . . . they also want to go a little sideways."

"Jesus!" Neary said.

"Longly," the dispatcher said, sounding bored. "Give us a location."

"Give me one, too," said Neary.

"It's over the Ingelside Elementary School heading northeast."

Roy yelled out the window, "Where's the Ingelside Elementary School . . . Anybody?"

"That's easy," said a guy, who was carrying a shotgun for some reason. "You go back to seventy, then—"

"No, wait a sec," Longly called. "Heading northwest on Daytona."

"Where's Daytona? Quick!"

"That's even easier." The gunslinger was seeing action now. "Okay, Jack, take any road out east of here till you get to city nine and farm eleven, but don't stop there 'cause there's a detour sign: 'Pardon Our Progress.'"

He was still going on as Neary shifted gears and backed away.

Five minutes later, Neary was lost on his own home ground. He was on some country road, surrounded by more of that insipid ground fog. Bumping over a rutted crossroads, the DWP truck stopped and Roy Neary shone his spotlight at a street sign. Shit! he checked the map again. *Shit!* Neary scooped out two troughs of Indiana clay as he ground the gears backward; he stopped again and spread the map over the steering wheel, twisting the little gooseneck lamp into bright submission.

Behind him a bank of lights from an approaching

vehicle lit up the rear window. They drew right up
behind Neary and stopped. The glare, bouncing off
his rear- and side-view mirrors, was almost as irritat-
ing as that municipal map with all of its myopic lines.
Absently, he stuck his hand out the side window and
waved the other vehicle around him.

For a moment, nothing happened. The intense light,
as if from a semi-truck's double-beams, now stung his
eyes. Impatiently now, he waved them around again.

Without a sound, moving at a slow, hypnotic pace,
the super high beams complied . . . rising *vertically*
out of sight, leaving darkness behind.

Intent on the map, Roy Neary had seen none of
this. His subconscious registered vaguely that the
bright lights were no longer bothering him. What
finally penetrated his consciousness was the noise. It
sounded like the rattling of tin. Neary looked up, then
around, and finally shone his spotlight on the road
sign.

It was vibrating so fast that the letters seemed to
multiply and superimpose. He looked again, unknow-
ingly making a "Huuuh?" sound. Next, the truck's
spotlight, dashboard lamp and headlights faded to a
faint amber glow and then went out.

Abruptly, the entire area for thirty yards around
him was assaulted by a silent explosion of the brightest
light imaginable. It was suddenly daytime. Neary tried
to look out his open window, but the light was too
bright and he had to duck back in. He felt an immedi-

ate burning, followed by a prickling sensation on the side of his face that he had been unwise enough to stick out the window. Neary went for the phone, but it was dead. The broadband radio had crackled out, too.

By now, Roy was too frightened to budge. Just his eyes moved. Then he threw his hands over his eyes and groped for his metal-rimmed sunglasses clipped to the visor above the windshield. He managed to get them on, and then—to his horror—found they were buzzing at his temples, vibrating as intensely as the road sign.

That was when the glove compartment, falling open at the hinges, began to rattle violently as everything metallic started sticking together. A box of paper clips popped open and dozens of the damn things flew past Neary's head and fastened themselves to the roof of the truck.

The sunglasses were too hot. They were burning his skin. Neary whipped them off his face and let them drop to the seat. Instead, they, too, flew past his head and stuck to the roof. He closed his eyes against the fierce light. The ashtray emptied itself out as though sucked weightless by a current of air from outside the truck and—

The hot light was gone. Paper clips rained down on Roy's head. He could no longer hear the sign shaking. He looked up and—for a second—saw the stars. Then, as if some tremendous tray were sliding out overhead, all the stars (except a few around the edges) were inked out by the limbo shape. Fluidly, the mass moved on and the stars started coming back out.

A distant rattling caused Neary to bring his head back inside and swing around in his seat. Suddenly his high beams, spot and lamp switched back on. Down the road there was a four-way stop. All four signs were dancing to and fro, vibrating so violently that metal around the signs' edges curled against the force. For a second the intersection was awash in that same blinding light. But for only a second. And in the dark, the signs were no longer vibrating.

All was still.

But when the radio blasted on, Neary screamed.

It was making noises that sounded like an electrical overload, and the voices weren't much better so far as Roy was concerned.

"I don't know. I'm asking *you*. Is there a full moon tonight?" came a police voice.

"That's a negative," the dispatcher, a female voice, said. "New moon on the thirteenth."

"Get out of here. Me and my partner are seeing this thing over Signal Hill. This is the thing everybody is screaming about. It's the moon . . ." There was a lot of static. "Wait a sec. Okay. It's starting to move now. West to east."

"This is Tolono Police," a new voice came on. "We are watching it, confirming it is definitely the moon. Be advised it is not moving. The clouds behind it are moving, giving it the illusion of movement over—"

"Where'd you study astronomy, Tolono?" a voice that Roy recognized as Longly's broke in. "When did you ever see clouds moving *behind* the moon?"

"What's your location?" the lady dispatcher asked wearily.

"Just off the Telemar Expressway and east toward Harper Valley."

"Oh, my God!" Roy Neary cried. "I know where that is."

Neary hit ninety-plus. He found himself entering a long, dark tunnel and as his high headlights cut through it, Roy became aware again of the prickling sensation on the side of his face. He also remembered how frightened he had been back there, and now here he was chasing after the thing that had so scared him. He really ought to stop, turn around and go back to Earl and the other guys. But, Neary realized, he was more excited than frightened now. He felt like a kid. It was too late to stop now. He was having too much fun. And so were the police.

"I see them, Charlie! I'm in pursuit."

"You can take it for what it's worth. These things were not manufactured in Detroit." That was Longly.

"It's decelerating. I don't know why it's decelerating, but it's getting closer. Three hundred yards."

"Can you catch up to it?" the dispatcher asked.

"I don't think so. About two hundred yards. That's it for me. I don't think we should rush into it."

"It's following all the S-turns. It's following all the roads."

"Radar shows 'em down to twenty-five miles per hour."

"Shit, that's a school zone they just passed through."

"Look at the traffic lights! They turn to green just as they get up to them."

A lot of static.

"Yes, sir . . . They're going right out east on Harper Valley."

Neary came out of the tunnel and rounded a curve at ninety-five miles an hour, traded paint with a guardrail, went into a skid and managed to correct without running off into the central divider gully. He shot past a sign: EAST HARPER VALLEY EXIT—3 MILES. Then Neary really stood on the accelerator, slowing only when the Harper Valley exit loomed up.

Skidding and braking, he whipped the truck off onto the exit road. It turned onto a two-lane country road, and Roy came down to a more cautious seventy.

Up ahead he thought he might have seen something on the—

A child!

Neary stood on the brakes. An instant later, a woman ran out onto the road and grabbed for the child. The truck was skidding wildly now as Roy fought the wheel. The woman and child were frozen in his headlights for another instant—yards, feet ahead, directly under the wheels.

Neary threw the wheel hard left, skidded by the

two bodies, and plowed into a snow fence, taking some of it with him before coming to rest.

For a long moment, everything was very still except for his panting breath. He switched off the engine. It took him three tries to get the door handle to work, so shaky were his arm muscles.

Neary finally staggered out of the high weeds and back to the center of the road. The woman stared blindly at him, her arms around the little boy, her hands over the boy's eyes, as if still shutting away from him the high, bright headlights bearing down upon them.

"Lady," Roy began, "you shouldn't let your little boy—"

"I've been searching for him for hours," Jillian Guiler burst out. "He wandered away from our house. I've been looking for hours. He just ran away. Hours and hours I've been—"

"Okay," Neary said. "Okay, I'm sorry I—"

"That's a dangerous curve," a voice said.

Neary turned to see—of all things—an old farmer sitting in a chair on the back of an ancient pickup. His family, a wife and two sons, were grouped around him, some with binoculars, one boy with a toy telescope.

"Just like the circus coming to town," the farmer was saying, taking a swig from a bottle of something. "They come through at night . . . they come through late so they don't disturb the residents."

A sudden wind sent Jillian's hair flying back from

her face. Roy could feel his own hair blown in the same direction. He turned to face the wind, whistling now through the snow fence.

In Neary's truck, tangled in yards of torn-up snow fence, the police radio talked on.

"Can you run a make on them?"

". . . I may be gaining again."

"As long as they keep following the road."

"This is Randolph County. We're monitoring you on the emergency frequency. What've you guys got down there?"

Squinting downwind, Neary could see something coming along the road, but it turned out to be a low-winged flight of birds, escaping something. Something on the horizon. Something that glowed.

A group of rabbits bounded past, ears flat against their heads.

"Here they come again," the farmer said.

Neary whirled back to stare down the road.

"Jesus!" he whispered to himself. "Jesus Chr—"

The very breath seemed to have been sucked out of his lungs. The vacuum was filled by a bass rumble, as though the air were being disturbed by lightning. Closing soundlessly on them at high speed was what looked like a sudden sunrise at two A.M., flying past him from east to west.

Without thinking, Roy covered his face with one arm and grabbed for the woman and the boy with the other. Jillian felt her face and neck burn, then prickle. The three clung tightly together as something like an Indian-summer sunset, flashing and blinking autumn colors, swept past them, slowly above the road ahead. A billboard featuring McDonald's golden arches was studied by six figures of light before the massive Christmas ornament moved on, a white spotlight picking out the dotted line on the road beneath it.

A third vehicle—resembling a jack-o'-lantern to Neary because there almost seemed to be a phantom face leering out of each of the bright lights, out of each of the thousands of little stained-glass colored sections—closed over, then passed them and following the road, made a right turn, signaled by three sequential directional lights flashing red like a T-bird.

Neary and Jillian were gasping with fright, but little Barry was jumping up and down, shouting, "Ice cream! Ice cream!" and laughing.

The old farmer, still sitting in his chair in the back of the pickup, said casually, "Yep, they can fly rings around the moon, but we're years ahead of 'em on the highway."

That was too much for Roy and Jillian. Their eyes locked, but they could think of nothing to say.

Neary swallowed, trying to get some words, some sounds, something out of his mouth. Something more was coming down the road. With a desperate shove, he threw himself, Jillian, and Barry off to the side of the road.

Just in time. Two police cruisers howled past at well over one hundred miles per hour.

Neary headed back to his truck.

"Stick around," the farmer said to him. "You should've seen it an hour ago."

"This is nuts," said Neary, just as another Indiana cruiser roared by.

"I may be drunk but I know I'm here," the old man shouted over the roar.

Barry was laughing again.

Neary got into the truck and started backing it out of the tangle of snow fence and high weeds. He spun his wheels in frustration, then calmed down and got the truck out of there.

"Where are we?" Neary asked Jillian.

"Harper Valley."

The truck took off.

"They just play," Barry said, snuggling up against his mother.

"What, Barry?"

"They play nice."

9

Accelerator jammed on the floor, Neary hunched close to the windshield, following the curves of the on-ramp and the glow ahead and above.

As he shot onto the highway, he heard the police calling to one another, although he did not yet have them in sight.

"I'm gaining on them, Bob!"

Roy's head was almost touching the glass. He moved back a moment and glanced down at the speedometer. Ninety-five, ninety-seven, ninety-nine.

". . . that's the Ohio tolls up there!"

Up ahead the flashing red and yellow lights of the last of the cruisers came into Neary's view. He had to slow slightly to hold on to the road as they swept around long bends. The formation of brilliant lights was still far ahead, sweeping smoothly around the bends as if the law of gravity was repealed.

In the distance, the line of tollbooths looked deserted to Neary. The normal bluish fluorescent light apparently blacked out here by the power failure, too.

At this hour of the night, there was little traffic between Indiana and Ohio.

At the tollbooths, one of the attendants was dozing
on his stool. The three flaming orbs soared smoothly
up and over the line of booths. All hell broke loose.
Red battery-operated alarm lights flashed on and off.
Sirens tore the stillness to pieces. The dozing attendant
jerked awake. Some dude was trying to get through
his tolls without paying! In the blink of an eye, the
first police cruiser shot through the gates. The second
cruiser whooshed past, sirens and roof lights crazy.
As the attendant started out of the booth to see what
the hell, the third cruiser displaced air, followed
closely by Neary's yellow DWP truck.

"I'm closing the gap," one of the policemen called.

"Man, you gotta see this. They're glued to the road!"
A hairpin curve was just ahead, and for the first time
since the pursuit began, the objects decided not to stay
glued to the road. They shot straight out over the
guardrail and into the air. An instant later, the police
officer, obviously locked in on the night lights and
doing at least eighty-five, followed them through the
guardrail and high into Ohio airspace for a sensational
moment before it pancaked into the embankment and
lost all its wheels and doors.

"DeWitt! You okay, DeWitt!"

The second patrol car seized the opportunity to
save itself and, brakes on fire, sideslipped right up to
the littered cliffside. Roy saw the two police officers

jump over the mangled guardrail and tear down the embankment to the creamed cruiser.

The third police cruiser tore after the speeding UFO with Neary hot in pursuit. Around curves, up grades, down hills the chase led. The visitor from another dimension glowed tantalizingly in the distance. Police sirens wailed unhappily.

Neary tooled his van on two wheels around a sharp turn. A Shell filling station stood to one side. Neary was about to roar past when the darkened station suddenly flared into brilliant daylight. Neary jammed on the brakes.

Three times the Shell station glowed. Three times it darkened. Neary grabbed for the spotlight on his van. He aimed it at the station's gas pumps. Then he clicked the brilliant searchlight on and off three times.

Madness erupted. The gumball machine at the entrance to the stationhouse began firing global bullets of gum in random directions. They pinged against gas pumps, windows, Neary's van.

The cigarette machine seemed to leap into the air and hang there, suspended in space. Packs of cigarettes swooped out and were sucked upward into the sky overhead.

The gas pump nearest to the van abruptly went insane. Its bell began ringing. The face of the pump showed a price of $1.17 per gallon. Suddenly, amid wild noise, the numbers clicked downward. The price dropped to fifty cents.

In celebration, all the gas pumps lifted their hoses and began spewing out fuel onto the concrete.

Overhead, Neary was aware, a dark shape seemed to hover, the focus of all this chaos. A pair of brilliant light beams blinded him for an instant as they shot down from the dark shape. They twiddled across the flooded concrete and passed over the telltale rubber tube that "bings" inside the stationhouse.

BING!

Pleased with this, the beam recrossed the tube. BING! It crossed back. BING! Now it broke into a flurry of movements, crossing recrossing.

BINGBINGBINGBINGBING!

Silence.

Almost before Neary realized it, the dark shape vanished. He put the van in motion. Sloshing through pools of gasoline, he resumed the chase. But it was over.

No fateful vision led the way through the flatlands of Ohio. In the distance, Neary could see the third police car paused by the side of the highway, obviously not sure what to do next. Finally, moving very slowly, it U-turned and came back to where the other cars had jumped the rail.

The third police car and then Neary, following, finally stopped. The other cops ran down the embankment while Neary looked up at the sky. Three firelights arced upward into a low-lying cloud bank. Once inside they turned the clouds to fire until the internal illumination gently faded restoring normal night again.

Neary turned back toward Indiana. The fluorescent lighting on both sides of the tollbooths was flickering back to life. Then Roy saw on the horizon a tapestry of light. A distant city was coming back on. Tolono? Harper Valley? It seemed the blackout was over.

As it turned out, Trooper Roger DeWitt was in better shape than his wrinkled cruiser. Sporting a broken nose, minor but multiple contusions and a possible concussion, he had strutted around the stationhouse for one hour telling everybody including drunk drivers, one male rape victim, and a dozen witnesses of that evening's skyjinks his version of God's truth. Now he was inside making his verbal report to Captain Rasmussen while in the State Highway Patrol processing room the other officers and Roy Neary were working up reports of their night to remember. It was now three thirty A.M., and Neary was fading. A man only has so many ounces of adrenaline, Neary thought. He craved a Mars Bar but would have settled for Mounds or M&M's. There weren't enough typewriters to go round, so Roy worked in pencil. He had a landslide of a headache.

"Got any aspirin?" he asked the room.

No one paid any attention to him.

"If Longly hadn't been with me," one of the troopers said to another, "I would have gone psychiatric."

Longly grinned. "I don't want to file this report," he said. "I want to publish it."

Just then, a door across the room burst open and

DeWitt emerged, limping, from the captain's office, closing the door behind him, but not before the captain had shoved through it. "It's enough to outrage common sense." The Captain addressed everyone in the processing room. "Ordinary people look to the police *not* to make bizarre reports of this nature."

"My knowledge is God's truth," DeWitt offered in his own defense.

"I will not see this department pressed between the pages of the *National Enquirer.*" Rasmussen looked at Longly and another trooper behind their typewriters. Again he spoke to the room. "When Flash Gordon and Buck Rogers are done, have them get their behinds in here."

He slammed out and the room fell stone quiet.

"Was he mad 'cause your car's gonna be a taxi next week?"

"Sweet Jesus." DeWitt now looked dazed as well as damaged. "I told him the whole thing. I didn't hold back nothing. The shooting stars. The speed. What the hell, I ain't no demolition derby . . . not on purpose."

"And?"

"He gave me a two-week suspension."

"*What?*" The other troopers stopped what they were doing and stared at the man.

"That's what I said." DeWitt started limping for the door. "Go try to tell somebody the truth and we'll all be watching TV in the daytime."

Roy watched the officers turn to their typewriters. He watched them reading over their respective reports. Some cops exchanged forced smiles. Then, as if some invisible puppeteer pulled simultaneously on five strings, five right hands reached into five typewriters and yanked out five N217 forms, crumpled them, and dropped them into wastebaskets.

"Go ahead, talk, mister," one officer said to Roy, smiling sheepishly as he inserted a new report form in his typewriter. "Be my guest."

Neary searched for a friend in the room and immediately understood the general situation. He got up and left.

In the Gobi, the wind rushes each morning to greet the sun. Grains of desert sand blow across rippled dunes as the thin orange-red edge of the sun appears in the east.

It summoned the wind this morning and, with it, a desert tribesman, burnoose drawn across his face to protect him from the stinging grains. Rifle across his legs, he let his camel find its own way along the trackless undulations.

Behind him, three more riders on camels squinted into the fiery heart of the dawn as if into the mouth of an opening furnace. The desert beasts moved with ungainly lurches, heavy saddlebags banging against their scabrous haunches.

Now the sun was halfway out of the horizon, a flaming semicircle that sent long shadows past each wavelike ripple of sand. The lead rider suddenly sat up in his saddle.

His camel dug all four hooves into the sand and let

out a spine-chilling scream, almost human. The rider pitched forward over the camel's head and hit the sand, somersaulting.

He knelt, staring wildly into the rising sun. Behind him, his three companions tried to rein in their beasts. Camels reared, pawed, backed, whinnied, and succeeded at last in toppling their riders.

The lead rider scrambled to his feet, retrieved his rifle, and began pawing among the heavy saddlebags. After a moment, he brushed sand from the face of an olive-drab radio transmitter. Hands trembling, he began manipulating dials and switches.

He blinked nervously and shouted something into the telephone handset connected to the radio. He listened, shouted again, and put the handset away.

Then he jumped to his feet. Waving his rifle, he rushed to his comrades. Squinting ferociously into the glare of the rising sun, they gestured, pointed, conferred. Now and then words seemed to fail them. They fell silent, staring in the direction of the sun.

At last they could hear a steady flat-flat-flat in the distance, growing louder. The leader glanced up at the sky. He pointed his rifle into the air and blindly fired off a shot, then another.

A light Loach recon helicopter bobbed over the nearest dune, rotors flat-flatting. Like a giant firefly, the two-man ship hovered above the camel riders, who gestured wildly, pointing toward the sun.

The Loach rose and fell, rose and fell. Then it settled slowly to the sand. Immediately other copters began to land in its wake. Men in military uniforms of no particular nation poured out of the ships. Some carried Nikons with long telephoto lenses. Others had mounted video cameras in shoulder braces. They moved warily to the end of the dune and stared down into the sun, an orange ball on the rim of the world.

Now Land-Rovers began to arrive, churning up long trails of dusty sand. The third vehicle swerved to a halt, all four tires milling sand. Lacombe stepped out, followed by Laughlin, his interpreter.

Tribesmen, photographers, pilots, and drivers turned in their tracks to stare at the gray-haired Frenchman. He stood beside his vehicle, the sun silhouetting him in a fiery outline. He stared where the rest of them had looked. Slowly, he removed his dark glasses.

He took a step in the direction all of them had been watching. Another step. A third. Then he stalked through the sand, pace quickening.

Brilliantly silhouetted by the sun, Lacombe's body suddenly moved into shadow. A huge shadow in the middle of the trackless Gobi desert spread its blackness over him.

He looked up, no longer squinting. High above him hung the gigantic bronze three-bladed screw of an oceangoing ship's propeller. Lacombe shaded his eyes as he stared upward.

"Another gift," he said. Suddenly, a drop of water oozed off the blade tip and dropped on his nose.

He recoiled, touched his nose, felt the wetness. Slowly, he touched his wet finger to his lips and tasted the water.

"Salt," he reported.

Chaos broke loose. Photographers scrambled over each other, aiming their lenses. Before them sat an immense oceangoing freighter fully five hundred thirty feet long. It lay on one side, steel plates dripping water.

Technicians began crowding forward. Scientists ran clicking Geiger counters over the dripping hull. Zoologists began prying barnacles from the plates. A crew with photographs and a thick book of engineering specs marched the length of the freighter from stem to stern.

"Danish," one of them remarked.

"Reported missing, with all hands aboard," another chimed in.

"Last seen near the island of Eleuthera," the first remembered.

"And no sign of flotsam or debris."

Silently, Lacombe stalked the heeled-over ship, but from a distance, staring up at its deck railings. At one point he turned to Laughlin. "Binoculars?"

His interpreter handed over a pair of field glasses. Lacombe peered through them, raking their line of sight slowly along the length of the ship.

"There!" she exclaimed. *"Regardez-la!"*

Laughlin squinted. "It's a giant circle."

The two men backed away from the damp ship until

they could see the circle more clearly. It seemed about twenty feet in diameter. Very clearly it was not part of the Danish freighter's original design.

Calling for ladders, Lacombe mounted the side of the ship and gingerly touched the edge of the circle. "Not paint," he called down. After a moment he descended to the sand.

"*Incroyable,*" he murmured. "The steel is deformed. It is as if a vast circle of suction had pulled the plates slightly up. Puckered the steel. Can you imagine a force so great that it can deform steel as easily as if it were damp paper?"

"But what caused it?" Laughlin demanded.

"I think, when we get this great tub on its keel," Lacombe told him, "we will find a matching circle on the opposite side of the ship. I think," he repeated for emphasis. "And if I am right, then we are dealing with something so huge and with such power that it can lift an oceangoing freighter as easily as you pick up an ice cube in a pair of tongs. *Comprenez-vous?*"

"*Bien sur,*" Laughlin murmured. "That is, not at all."

"We must calculate the latitude and longitude of this spot most accurately, *n'est-ce pas?* We must know it precisely."

"That's being done already."

The Frenchman nodded. "You see," he said after a moment, "we know nothing at all. Except for one thing."

"Yes?"

The two men stared at the immense hulk. Now the

morning sun was high over the horizon. Heat waves made the air flicker and tremble. Scientists and photographers swarmed over the ship like feasting ants.

"We know it is another gift," Lacombe said then. "And, in time, we will know . . . why."

10

It was after four A.M. by the time Neary got home. From somewhere he had inhaled a new burst of energy while charging down the hall to the bedroom, shouting "Ronnie! Ronnie!" Neary couldn't control himself, every muscle was vibrating from an unforeseen reserve of adrenaline. He was nauseated from all the excitement and his second word almost blew Ronnie out of bed.

"Honey, wake up."

Her two blue eyes filled with terror, her long blond hair sprang tangled with sleep.

"What's it, kids . . . and fire, wh—?"

"It's okay, kids are okay," he said again. "Honey, you won't believe this."

Ronnie caught her breath and stared at the luminous clock dial. "Right. I don't believe you're waking me up at ten minutes after four."

"You're not going to believe what's happening."

"I'm not listening," Ronnie said distinctly, and pulled the covers over her head.

"You don't have to listen." Roy's breathing reminded Ronnie of the way little Toby would wolf down dessert. "They don't make any noise at all. There was nothing but air and all of a sudden, whoosh . . . then whoosh . . . then a little red whoosh . . . Jesus!"

From under the covers Ronnie absorbed the whooshes before remembering. "The Department's been trying to reach you. They couldn't reach you . . ."

"Yeah, I know. I shut my phone off."

She started to wake up. "Roy, you shouldn't do that. They have to talk to you . . . all kinds of crazy things are going on. The phone has been ringing off the hook. I remember now. They want you to call them now!"

Neary saw that words weren't enough so he used two hands to pull his wife out of bed.

"Come on! Get outta bed. What do you want to wear, dammit? The sun's gonna put the stars out."

"Roy! What are you talking about."

"Nothing. I'm not talking nothing until you see 'em yourself. Ronnie, oh, Ronnie. This is so important. I need you to see this with me. I really need you with me now."

Ronnie saw no humor in his face and softened immediately. "Well, we can't leave the kids."

"The kids, yeah, the kids . . . kids!! kids!!"

While he prodded his family into their clothes and out of the house, Neary collected cameras, binoculars, opera glasses and blankets.

"Are we going to a drive-in?" Brad asked, still half-asleep.

"You stole my luminous paint," Toby remembered.

"You'll get your luminous paint!" Neary was jubilant. "Everything's going to be luminous!"

He got everyone as far as the kitchen, where Ronnie diverted to the refrigerator. She opened the door and grabbed her raw vegetable pouch. The refrigerator light was an unappetizing green, and Toby said, "That green light makes me barf."

"I'll change it after I lose another three pounds," his mother told him for the twentieth time.

Neary started hustling them all out of the house again and toward the family's Chevy station wagon parked around the back of the driveway.

"Roy." Ronnie was leaking steam. "You've proved your point. We all got out of the house. Now can we go back to bed?"

Instead of answering, Neary started shoving the children inside the car.

"This is only funny if it ends here in the driveway," Ronnie said, going around to her side of the car.

"You promised Goofy Golf," Toby said from the middle seat. His eyes were already closed again.

Finally, everyone was in. Ronnie had not closed her door and the ceiling light inside the car was still on. For the first time Ronnie saw it: Neary was red on one half of his face. Bright red.

"Roy, what is that? You're sunburned."

Neary peered into the rear-view mirror. This visible evidence made him even redder. "Holy shit," he whispered. "I guess I took my vacation while you were sleeping."

"But it's only half your face."

But Neary was already backing down the driveway, returning to where the excitement had been most extreme.

He drove quickly to the place where it had all happened, pulled off the road and stopped near the scattered snow fence. The farmer and his family were gone, leaving behind some Colonel Sanders' boxes and one bottle of Wild Turkey.

Ronnie and the kids sounded like a sleeping symphony of adenoid troubles. But Roy was on point. He kicked circles for a while in the cool early morning, waiting . . . waiting for what? Waiting for the experience to come again. Please come again, he thought to himself. Why had something that was so frightening become so enthralling? He wanted seconds but now the dark was playing tricks.

The police weren't with him now. He was alone out here. Did they like people who waited alone? Was it easier to get away when—?

Something woke Ronnie. She glanced back and saw her three children snoring against one another. And then there was her husband pacing back and forth nervously, eyes skyward. She got out, closing the car door softly, and fell into step.

"What are we doing here, Roy? Why won't you tell me what you're waiting for?"

"You'll know it when you see it," he told her without confidence.

"Come on," Ronnie said. "I came here with you. I'm taking this very well. Now tell me. What did it look like?"

Roy waited, stared up and down the road, watched the sky a moment longer, then: "Kind of . . . like an ice cream cone."

This was almost too much for Ronnie. "What flavor?" she asked with murderous innocence.

But Neary took her seriously. "Orange. It was orange . . . and it wasn't really like an ice cream cone . . . it was sort of in a shell . . . this . . ." He made sculpting motions with both hands.

"Like a taco?"

"No, rounder, larger . . . and sometimes . . . it was like . . . like . . . you know, those rolls we had yesterday?"

"Bran muffins?"

"No! Not for breakfast—" Neary was conscious that his wife was humoring him and also running out of humor, but he persisted anyway. "For dinner. What were those rolls? Those curvy ones?"

"You mean the crescent rolls?" she exclaimed, as though dealing with a Romper Room student.

"Yeah!" he said, excited all over again. "And it gave off a kind of neon glow."

That was definitely too much for Ronnie. She reached into her Baggie for a carrot. Neary walked a few paces away from her munching and hunched down near a rock, eyes heavenward again. Ronnie watched him anxiously. Obviously Roy was going through something . . . something she couldn't begin to understand, but, apparently, it was important to him. Maybe she had been too bitchy.

Ronnie approached Roy and used her favorite Little Miss Marker voice. "Don't you think I'm taking this really well?"

He didn't answer but stood up, still looking at the stars starting to fade in the ever lightening sky.

Ronnie looked up too and gave a little shudder. She didn't know why, but she was slightly frightened. It was all a little weird. A lot weird.

"Snuggle," she said to him.

Neary dutifully put his arm around her and drew her to him. Ronnie put her arms around his waist and began to nibble his ear.

"I remember when we used to come to places like this to look at each other." She said it like Bambi.

Neary looked down at her and, seeming to remember some good old times, he smiled. Ronnie smiled back and gently sucked on Roy's upper lip. He had always gone for that in a big way, and soon their kisses spread inside. But Roy was not so engrossed that he couldn't weasel open half an eye and turn it to the skies. Because that's precisely when everything exploded with a blue-hot fire-whoosh that tore at his clothes. Neary almost jumped out of his skin as the red lights diminished in the distance, but Ronnie knew it was only a semi-truck-trailer, and after a few seconds so, glumly, did Roy.

The spell was broken.

Ronnie, testing her husband, asked, "If one of those things came down right now and the door opened, would you go on it?"

Roy, thrilled at the proposition, cried, "Jesus Christ, yes!" Then, seeing and feeling the hurt tense through her, he added, "Well, anyone would."

But the damage was done. Ronnie broke away from him, and went back toward the car. He hurried after her.

Ronnie stopped and turned on him. "You know what you've done to us?" she cried out. "You know what this means? You've brought us out here twenty miles from home in the middle of the night . . . and you destroyed our sleep cycle. Your sons are gonna conk out in the middle of the day and Sylvia will be up until one A.M. for the next three nights because their father swears he saw a flat, orange Betty Crocker crescent roll that flies. We might as well all have breakfast right now."

She paused to catch her breath and then in a lower tone, completed the demolition. "Don't ever try anything like this again. We're your family. It is not normal."

There was nothing that Ronnie could have said, Neary knew, that could have been more final. It sure wasn't normal, but as Neary was about to discover, normality, as he once knew it, was coming to an end.

11

There is no fast way to get to Benares. The ancient and most holy city of the Hindus is approachable mainly through faith.

An approach by military aircraft was out of the question. To have sent a fighter plane or attack bomber through India's airspace would not only have freaked out the militantly neutral Indians but, more important, would have endangered the secrecy of the project.

David Laughlin supposed, privately, that if there had been time, Lacombe would have traveled to Benares in the proper manner, on bare feet, wearing a loincloth and supported by a wooden staff. As it was, Laughlin was grateful for the small, fourteen-passenger Corvette jet borrowed from Air Alsace, which made the trip from Paris to Rangoon in just half a day.

A Vertol chopper brought them in low over the spires and domes of Benares a half hour later, as the sun was setting. The river moved sluggishly beneath the helicopter, its holy waters freighted with the holiest of silt.

The hillside lay a few miles outside the city. The Vertol hovered at a discreet distance while its pilot tried to find a place to land. It wasn't easy.

"Look at them!" Laughlin said. "Thousands!"

"Tens of thousands," Lacombe corrected.

"It's fantastic. I—"

"The sadhu is a very holy man," Lacombe cut in quietly, above the rotor noise. "But also very practical. He also wants an answer. In his lifetime. He has been listening for many years. With him it is more than a matter of faith. It is a matter of results."

Laughlin thought that over. "But I thought the Hindus went the other way," he shouted. "Nirvana, not here."

Lacombe shrugged.

The chopper set down gently in a space near two Mercedes tour buses. The pilot cut the engines and the rotors whined down. Dust started settling over everything within a hundred yards. Lacombe climbed out first and stood momentarily in the brilliant sunset with Laughlin and two technicians.

The blood-red orange rays of the sun were coming in almost horizontally now. In a little while the great hot ball of flame, filtered and distorted by endless miles of dusty atmosphere, would swell, darken and hide itself from sight behind the low range of hills to the west.

"Let us go," Lacombe said.

Laughlin gestured to the two technicians, who

picked up their microphones, Nagra tape recorder, portable battery-belts, and the lightweight Arriflex 16-mm camera. The four men moved slowly through the crowd of pilgrims.

The people were densely packed, some on small rugs, with baskets of food beside them. There were whole families, even ancient-looking grandparents (who were probably under forty years of age), wizened and emaciated by hunger and disease.

The Westerners moved with prudent speed up the hillside toward the cleared area where the sadhu sat, legs crossed beneath him in the lotus position, eyes shut, palms pressed together, elbows out to the side like some strange, meditative bird of passage.

A sleek young Brahmin in city whites arose at Lacombe's approach. Laughlin moved in to translate while the technicians began setting up.

"It lacks half an hour of the sun's death," the Brahmin told Lacombe.

His accent bothered Laughlin: smooth, Oxonian English. The young man wore well-shined chukka boots, pipestem-thin trousers of white muslin, and a collarless jacket of the same fabric. He looked too urbanized for this place, his smooth flow of talk too glib. But even the holiest of men, Laughlin thought, needed managers.

The sadhu himself moved not a muscle. By not even the flicker of an eyelid did he acknowledge anything around him of this world. Lacombe stood in contemplative silence for a moment, then lowered himself to a lotus seat near, but at a respectful distance from, the sadhu.

The microphones were ready now, each in its parabolic reflector. The Arriflex was to be hand-held. Lacombe had insisted that it not be mounted on a tripod. He wanted the technician to keep it on his shoulder, to have the mobility to photograph . . . whatever there was to photograph.

His eyes closed, the Frenchman seemed to relax, although his back was stiffly erect. Out of the corner of his mouth, in French, he murmured an order to Laughlin, who turned to the audio technician.

"He wants to make sure you shield the Nagra."

"Why?" the man wanted to know. "We're nowhere near any electrical interference."

"He's had bad luck before with tape recordings. The capstan motor usually conks out and the recording heads lose magnetism."

"No kidding," the technician said. "Well, if he says so." He produced a large, copper-mesh, boxlike affair, a shield that he placed over the small precision Nagra recorder. Then, shoving copper spikes into the earth, he grounded the shield carefully. "Does that suit the mother?"

Laughlin wondered, and not for the first time, what they were doing in this strange place, with all these thousands, waiting . . . waiting for what? The report spoke of an event strictly unbelievable, but Lacombe had shown him how to suspend disbelief, to open himself to the incredible.

Laughlin turned away and watched the bloated disk of the sun as the hills to the west began biting a chunk out of its lower rim. In a moment only half the sun was visible. The sadhu stirred slightly.

What happened next seemed to be in slow motion to Laughlin. He watched the sadhu's outturned elbows pull in toward his emaciated brown ribcage. The palms of his hands, still pressed together, began a slow separation until only the fingertips still touched.

The sadhu's eyelids slowly rose, like shutters on temple windows. Open, his eyes were enormous, jet black, ringed all the way around by white, the white then ringed by glossy black lashes.

The sadhu's body stirred. Slowly, without apparent effort, he began to rise from the lotus to a standing position. The sleek city Brahmin sank to his knees, Laughlin found himself sitting down abruptly, as if the only person who had any right to be on his feet was the sadhu. Out of the corner of his eye, Laughlin could see the audio technician and the camera operator, fall, incredibly, to their knees. He was sure they had no idea what they were doing.

With grave deliberateness, the sadhu's bare arms spread out from his body like the powerful wings of some great land-locked bird ready to take the skies. Behind him, all that was left of the sun was the thinnest edge of rind. As Laughlin watched, the sun snuffed out. Darkness fell instantly.

The sadhu's long arms swung up at his sides to shoulder height. They paused, then continued their upward sweep until the gnarled backs of his hands touched each other high over his head. They paused again. Then he brought the arms down in one great sweep—a conductor cueing a mighty orchestra.

From ten—twenty—thousand throats came a low, melodious note. They sustained it with such power that it began to eat its way into Laughlin's brain. He noticed Lacombe's eyes snap open and swing sideways, cursing the technicians. Laughlin gestured. The audio man started the Nagra. Laughlin could see its reels turning through the copper mesh.

Now the sadhu brought his arms up and cued another note, an interval above the first, higher on the scale. His worshippers filled the world with the two tones, alternating them, sounding them separately and together—a minor interval, Laughlin thought, less than a third. A minor third? Not quite.

The sadhu produced another note and then another and another. Now Laughlin began to lose a sense of the melody in the harsh cacophony of many voices. The ground beneath him seemed to vibrate with the intensity of the notes, unmelodic, strange to Western ears, notes the report had stated had come down from the stars four nights ago and that the sadhu and his followers had been sounding each night since.

The intervals were never whole, Laughlin felt. They were quartered, halved, bent slightly into microtone steps. Each singer changed the notes slightly, making a raw, elemental howl. It soared skyward in a great chant, somehow ominous. It shook the earth beneath Laughlin but it also made the air itself vibrate.

The tropical twilight was now night. Damp blackness had descended upon them all. And even though they could no longer see their sadhu, the many thousands continued their chant, forcing it to grow to an almost unbearable intensity.

The stars had come out overhead. Laughlin gazed upward, shaking with the fierceness of the singing around him. He watched the star at the end of the Big Dipper's handle. It grew brighter, waned, brightened again. There was a frequency to it, like a message in Morse code. And then it . . . exploded.

A bright crimson flash illuminated the upturned faces of the multitude. Lacombe was on his feet now, standing beside the sadhu. The cameraman had swung his shoulder-braced Arriflex upward.

The crimson light elongated into a rolling pillar, turned orange. Then yellow. Then pale green. It hovered in the sky, and suddenly the heavens were filled with the same five notes. The same chord, played on something that was not human. Pure. Melodic. Clean. The worshippers below fell silent. And once again the sky sang down to them.

"Goddamn!" the cameraman said.

The pillar of fire winked out. The song ended.

The worshippers below sank back, faces pressed to the earth. The sadhu turned to Lacombe.

"The sky," he said in a thin voice, "the sky sings to us."

The two men embraced. Tears ran down the Frenchman's cheek. His voice was thick with emotion.

"It sings to all of us, my friend."

12

Several hours later that morning, Saturday, Neary stood bleary-eyed in front of the bathroom mirror, trying to organize enough of himself to at least get the razor working. Eventually, Roy took the can of Rapid Shave and nozzled a mound of white lather into the palm of his right hand. He automatically lifted the cream mountain toward his face when something mind boggling stopped him.

Neary began to stare at the stuff in his hand. He cocked his head and brought the lather mound eye level, then vaguely began to shape some of it with the middle finger of his left hand.

"No, that's not right," Neary said to himself, not really conscious of what he was doing or saying. But this image was reminding him of something—something maddeningly out of mental reach—he knew this shape so well and yet it felt as if the connection was a million miles away. Neary blinked, a little distressed. Everybody experiences something like this he thought —a moment that feels so familiar, a face you think

you've seen before but really never have, a place you
think you visited once but knew you never did. These
were flashes that some psychoanalysts like to call *déjà
vu*; they always passed in a few seconds. This flash
was sure taking its time passing. It lingered for minutes, and so did Neary's eyes on that sloppy mound of
Rapid Shave. Then . . .

The appearance of Ronnie—in the mirror—standing
in the bathroom doorway brought Roy partway back.

"Ronnie," he said. "What does this remind you of?"

She totally ignored the lather mound, and said
firmly, "We're going to tell people at the party tonight
that you fell asleep under a sunlamp on your right
side."

"What? What for?"

"I don't want to hear you talking about it at the
party," she said. "Not till you know what you're talking
about."

"If I don't talk about it," he said, essaying logic,
"how am I gonna find out what's to know?"

"Talk about it with your buddies in the Department, not at parties."

"What does the Department know?"

During this meeting of the minds, Brad and Toby
had wandered into the bathroom.

"Dad, are they for real?" Brad asked.

"No, they're not for real," Ronnie snapped.

"Don't tell him that," Neary said.

"Mom . . . I believe in them," Brad persisted.

"No, you don't."

"Dad says so."

"He does not," Ronnie said. Then, pleadingly, "Roy?"

"I just want to know what in the world is going on," Neary admitted, the mound of foam still balanced in his right hand.

"It's just one of those things," Ronnie said, matter-of-factly, as if that resolved everything.

"Which things?"

"I don't want to hear about this anymore."

"Do they live on the moon?" Toby asked.

"They got bases on the moon," Brad said, really getting into it, "so at night they can come in your window and pull the covers off!"

Ronnie shut her eyes. "I'm not listening to this. I don't hear it."

"Last night," Neary said, as calmly as he could, "I saw something I can't explain."

Her fierce blue eyes snapped open and she fixed him in the mirror with her glare. "Last night, at four A.M., I saw something I can't explain. A grown man—" Ronnie stopped abruptly, sensing the boys' full attention.

"Ronnie, you know I'm going out there again tonight, damn it!"

She turned to leave, and said lightly, "No, you're not."

"Yes," he said, with a dramatic pause, "I am."

The phone began ringing.

Ronnie turned back, and said, playfully again, "No,

you're not." She reached into the bathroom, grabbed his right wrist and planted his palm upward into his face. The shaving foam gooshed and Neary looked like a bathtub toy.

Roy stared at himself in the mirror. The white foam emphasized the reddish color of his cheek. He smeared some of the foam onto his chin and other cheek. "It ain't a moonburn, goddamn it," he muttered to himself.

Neary had started shaving when Ronnie reappeared in the mirror. She looked as if she had just been told something awful. Tears began to come out of her eyes and she just stood there in the doorway shaking.

Roy turned around immediately, saying, "Okay, Ron . . . I don't have to go."

"R-Roy," she said, "that was Grimsby, from the Department."

"Huh?"

"You're fired, Roy." Ronnie was really sobbing now and she collapsed into his arms, cheek against cheek, tears and lather. "They . . . he wouldn't even talk to you. What are we going to do? You got fired? What's going on?"

"Jesus!" Neary said, stunned. He's just stood there, razor in one hand, face smeared like a real bozo, his wife sobbing against him, looking at everything in the mirror and seeing none of it.

"Roy, what are we going to do?"

Neary, still stunned, didn't really hear her. His eyes, fixed in space, finally focused on a white object that he saw through the open bathroom door in the bed-room. It was a pillow on their bed. It had been left in a pushed-together, lumpy shape just like the shaving cream earlier.

"No," Neary muttered to himself. "That's not right."

13

He'd gone back the next night. Of course. And when none of the strange objects or colors appeared, he swore he was going to give up the whole idea. But the night after that he returned again.

The people he found there were getting to know one another. Old friends. The farmer in his pickup, with his pint bottle of whiskey, was on hand. So was a lady who had brought along a rocker and sat there doing needlepoint, to fill in the time before the next appearance of what everybody had taken to calling "the night things." Another elderly woman had an album of photographs of "them," the by-product of other nights in other places. A sound made everyone look toward the northern skies. Jet aircraft could be heard passing in the rarefied distance. "We'll be here all night if that keeps up," one of the elderly people complained. Roy knelt down by a lady who was eighty if she was a day. "Are they coming over tonight?" he whispered gently. Those words were like magic, for her very pressed face blossomed years off her, as though Neary had told her the meaning of life. She became teary-eyed, saying, "Oh, I hope so. Don't you?"

"Yes," he answered her in all seriousness. The old lady measured his fervor, blinked an eye and hefted to her lap a leatherette volume-sized photo album. She opened it to the first page.

"I took these myself," she said smartly. "Out by the parochial school."

Neary looked at her six color snapshots, a splash of yellow, a slit of white, a blur of out-of-focus blue. Anybody who didn't know how to use a camera produced mistakes like that for the first few rolls of film.

It wasn't that they were kooks, the kind of crazies who were always sighting flying saucers. It was just that, except for her, Neary didn't sense in any of them the same yearning need he had to find out what had happened. They seemed content simply to witness it, like the crowd at the circus that watches the fire-eater spew great sheets of flame but doesn't care how he does it.

The second night after the "night things" had appeared, quite a crowd seemed to have collected. There were people Neary couldn't remember seeing before. And, for the first time, he noticed the young woman and her little boy whom he'd pulled from the path of the wildly careening police cruisers.

Neary nodded to her over the heads of the crowd. She took her boy's hand and came over. "You do remember us?"

"How can I forget?"

"Jillian Guiler," she said, shaking his hand. "This is Barry."

"Roy Neary. That was some night, wasn't it?"

"It doesn't feel like it's over." She touched his cheek. "You're sunburned."

"Hoping to tan the other side tonight."

"It got my face and neck." She opened her blouse to reveal the upper curve of her breasts and the hollow at the base of her throat.

She watched as Roy's cheek turned a shade darker. "I'm sorry," she said, buttoning up. "I just had the feeling you were my oldest friend." She laughed. "It only takes one experience like that, doesn't it?"

Neary nodded, no longer embarrassed. As he did so, a genial-looking man in unmatching slacks and a sports jacket shone a flashlight on them. Their sunburns seemed to stand out in his beam. This seemed to please him, and with a Pentax and strobe, he snapped their picture. Jillian blinked and turned toward him as the man focused at little Barry, sitting near the fence and playing with a mound of dirt.

Moving swiftly, Jillian got in the way of the amateur photographer. "He's a little young to have a record," she told him angrily.

Neary watched the man cough up an apology and ankle away. "Where do you think he's from?"

"Earth," Jillian muttered bitterly. She bent down to wipe dirt off Barry's face. He was busily patting together a tall, conical mound.

"I, uh, have three of my own at home," Neary announced.

"Did you tell your wife about what we saw?"

"Of course."

"What does she think?" Jillian asked.

"She understands," Neary said with some sarcasm, "perfectly."

Jillian grinned. "I called my mother to tell her. She said that's what I got for living alone." She paused, and Neary saw that in some way she felt embarrassed, as he had before at the sight of the breasts—well, part of them.

"I'm not alone at all," she covered quickly. "There's Barry and the neighbors and I'm . . . not really . . . alone at all."

"Barry's father?"

"Died." She paused. She looked away from him. "I don't suppose he'd have understood this any better than your wife does."

There was nothing Neary could think of to say at this point. Instead he hunkered down to Barry's level and helped him pat dirt into place. "Working kind of late tonight, huh, kiddo?"

"I know he should be in bed," Jillian said in a guilty tone. "But after the way he ran off the other night, I'm not letting him out of my sight."

Neary nodded. He stared for a moment at the cone of dirt the little boy had built. He fingered a twig and etched fluted sides into the mound. "Hm." He reached for some pebbles nearby. "Try these," he offered.

Barry arranged them around the base of the cone, as if they were boulders thrown there by some explosion of natural forces.

"That's better," Neary said. Oddly enough both the boy and his mother accepted this as perfectly natural behavior.

"Hey," Neary asked, suddenly puzzled. "What does this remind you of?"

Jillian dug deep for an answer but she didn't know what. Then she bent over Barry to gently rough up the smooth side facing her. "I like it better like so," she said.

"Me, too," he breathed.

"Here they come!" a voice shouted.

"Out of the northwest!" someone yelled.

Neary and Jillian looked in the direction everyone was pointing. A hush descended over all. Adults and juveniles raised binoculars and cameras. On somebody's transistor radio the Eagles were singing "Desperado."

"There!" Jillian said pointing.

Two foggy pinpoints of light shifted back and forth, rising, falling, growing brighter in the darkness.

Neary raised his camera. "I'm ready this time."

She had placed her hand on his arm. "You're trembling."

"I know." Neary laughed recklessly. "What if we're just two whackos standing on a hill with a dozen other loonies?"

"Your eyes burn, don't they?"

"For two days now."

"Mine, too."

"But this is crazy," he said, his teeth almost chattering. "It's like Halloween for grown-ups."

The lights were bearing down on them inexorably now, blinding, larger, merciless, painful to watch. "Trick or treat?" Jillian asked then.

Nearly aimed his camera, but he had begun shaking so badly he wondered what kind of picture he'd get. "If those things stop and open their doors," he asked her, "would you get in and go?"

"If those things stop, I'm going home."

"Listen," Neary said. "The sound . . . listen."

The gathering in the field stirred as an unusual sound came over them, permeating the air. It was a rhythmical noise, blowing against the wind—louder now. And suddenly it was coming faster and more frenzied than any of them had expected, and fear shot through them all as they tried and failed to interpret the internal combustive pounding and . . . two blinding anticollision lights swallowed their world. The very air was displaced. And with the sky like summer noon, the lights suddenly gave way, clearly revealing two Air Force Huey helicopters that descended howling upon pockets of the idle curious, beating on them with hot air, gas exhaust, sucking dirt, napkins and other debris up into the spiraling convections, and still the screaming machines maneuvered around each other until even aluminum chairs, card tables, blankets, and picnic leavings were sent up and distributed to the next county.

In dismay, in self-disgust, and in some anger, too, he watched the two Air Force helicopters hover a dozen feet above them.

Neary saw the little old woman with the snapshots as she chased after them, whirling wildly in the wash from the two choppers, whose beams blinded her.

Barry screamed. He jumped and began to run. Jillian grabbed him. "Barry, it's only helicopters, Barry."

"Yeah," Neary shouted over the noise and dust. "They're ours."

The downwash from the rotors had set a road sign trembling. Neary watched it vibrate for a moment, just as the road sign had vibrated that other night. Then it had seemed wild, supernatural, something caused by . . . well, perhaps by night things.

Now he could see quite plainly that a sign was vibrating in the harsh wind of a maneuvering helicopter. It was happening right here in front of a hundred witnesses.

And for the first time in this whole insane affair, Neary began to doubt not only what he'd seen, but what he'd thought about it.

14

Out here in the desert the stars were big and hard as diamonds. Some of the stars closest to the horizon scintillated from all the rising heat released after another desert scorcher.

It was midnight in Barstow, California, and the monstrous parabolic ear of the Goldstone Radiotelescope was listening to the sky. Station 14 was down for overhaul. That was the cover story. But the same 210-foot dish that tracked the Viking, Helios, Pioneer, Mariner, Jupiter, Saturn, and Voyager missions was honed in on a state vector in "deep space." Inside the blockhouse a sign barked to all who entered: NETWORK DATA PROCESSING ACTIVITIES. ON-DUTY OPERATION PERSONNEL ONLY! CONTACT MC COPSCON 5883. A handprint Ident. box blocked a vacuum-sealed doorway like a sentry. There was a lot of anxiety on this special night. Six right hands pressed down on the sentry box, handprint identifications were made, and the door hissed open. It looked more like a storage area than the mission control computing center. The core of activity was a geodesic cubicle that rested on a flatbed trailer in the center of this otherwise dark and empty warehouse. Inside, the cubicle looked like a college fraternity prank. Two dozen project members were scrunched up to their shoulders in CRTs, telemetry tracking hardware, command function consoles, transmitter and receiving units, and, most incongruous of all, a mini-Yamaha synthesizer and Claude Lacombe doing a five-note exercise on its keyboard. It seemed as if he was sending a message. His fingers touched staccato, but the sound was undeniably India. Benares. The sky music. It was finally serving its hypothetical purpose.

And then came the response. The CRT readout was flooded with it. The hardcopy poured out of an IBM in reams. The paperwork was all over the floor, and project members were all thumbs trying to read it. It wasn't coming back. It was numbers. For fifteen minutes there occurred a rush of pulses that dotted the paper. There were pauses and long intervals and then more rapid-fire communications. Lacombe was certain of that. Communication was taking place. He sat down and pressed his forehead to the palms of his hands. He took a breath and expelled the air, shuddering. The teletype noise was deafening to some of the younger people in this claustrophobic space, but when the chattering stopped it was Lacombe's heart that sank. Only when the communication resumed would the Frenchman settle back and almost smile.

"Okay, gang!" It was the operations advisor who

was speaking now. "Here's the pattern. We've received two fifteen-minute broadcasts. One hundred and four rapid pulses before a five-second pause, then, forty-four pulses and another five seconds' rest, then thirty RPs and a sixty-second interval before an entirely different set of signals, which go as follows: forty plus five. Thirty-six plus five. Ten, then sixty, rest, and back to a hundred and four."

Lacombe played the five notes into the transmitting equipment, and a Cal Tech advisor was quick to ask, "What about a response to that?" Lacombe looked up at him and shrugged. Maybe tomorrow they would learn what the notes meant. But now, the race was on, and twenty-four mission advisors became think-tank executives.

One shaggy-headed man spoke first as he sorted through the repeated numbers. "It's not my social security number. Too many digits."

Somebody else quipped, "Maybe it's how many Quarter Pounders Ronald McDonald sold last month."

Everybody laughed at this except Lacombe. He didn't understand the joke and looked to his interpreter for the translation. But Laughlin didn't respond. He wasn't even looking at his employer, but instead was up to his armpits in hardcopy. Lacombe studied him. Laughlin was in a sweat over something, and when he looked up everyone was looking the other way. Everyone but Lacombe. The Frenchman nodded to his interpreter, encouraging him to say what was on his mind. Laughlin did just that.

"Excuse me!"

Everyone was pondering the big question and talking amongst themselves, so Laughlin screwed on his lumberjack voice and overdid it slightly. "EXCUSE ME!"

The room fell silent. Even the readouts stopped printing. Ironically, it was the end of a receiving cycle.

"Uh . . . before I got paid to speak French, I got paid to read maps and that number looks like a longitude to me."

Nobody budged. Laughlin's opinion drew blank stares. So he went on. "Two sets of three numbers, right? Well, the first number's got three digits, the last two are below sixty."

Laughlin stood up and moved to join Lacombe. Lacombe was already on his feet ready to burst loose with Eurekas! The room remained in a stupefied silence. Then, as everyone grappled with the idea, a core of excitement formed in the center of the group and rippled outward.

"Maybe . . ." someone spoke out, "maybe they're telling us a location in right ascension and declination on the sky. Maybe giving us galactic coordinates."

"No way, man," someone was quick to say. "That doesn't correspond to the direction of our 'Big Ear.' I think the man's right! I think we're getting terrestrial coordinates." And that was the pin buster.

Every project official was screaming for a map. A burst of manpower left the audio cubicle and raced to the corridor, heading for the mission supervisor's office.

Inside the office a large globe rested in its steel cradle. Suddenly the door flew open and the hallway light spilled in. Dawn broke on Rand McNally's western hemisphere, and excited project members rushed in like teenagers vandalizing the principal's office. They tried to move the globe in its stand, but it must have weighed three hundred pounds. A mathematics wizard used his shoulders to pop the globe from its moorings and bobble it back into the corridor.

Other members formed a relay team, and planet Earth, tossed like a volleyball, rounded a corner and flew toward the communications cubicle. Once inside, Laughlin slapped away the extra fingers and traced the longitude from the South Pole.

"Antarctica, ocean . . . ocean . . . ocean . . . just missing Easter Island, just missing Sala-Y-Gomex Island. Landfall in Mexico. Just missing Puerto Vallarta . . . crossing into New Mexico and picking up Carlsbad Caverns but continuing on and—"

Another man's fingers started tracing another line westward across the heartland of the United States. "Maine . . . New Hampshire . . . Great Lakes . . . Minnesota . . . South Dakota—"

And then their fingers came together in the northeast corner of the state of—

"Wyoming?" Laughlin looked up at Lacombe. "Wyoming." The silence was shattered by the Texas drawl of the team leader.

"Well, what are we waiting for, get me a geodetic sectional map of Wyoming. Get me everything on it!"

Meanwhile Lacombe sat back down, donned his headphones, played the five musical tones into the great transmitter and waited, listening. Nothing. He keyed the Yamaha again. Nothing. Lacombe sat forward, intently. He played again, but this time the sounds were all but drowned out by two-dozen project members celebrating their first definitive breakthrough.

15

The toy xylophone was poorly tuned. That was why the five notes sounded so strange when little Barry played them.

He didn't learn them all at once, Jillian noted from the other room. He had kept working on the tune until he got it . . . well . . . the way he wanted it.

To Jillian's ear, even though the tune was strange, Barry's chuckles were reassuring. He was there. He was happy. The tune's curious sequence of five notes —where do kids get these ideas?—was oddly disturbing, but of course these toy xylophones were never accurate. It was easy to make them sound . . . well . . . peculiar.

Jillian had spent the day, as she had the day before, making endless charcoal and pastel sketches. She had abandoned a career in art by the simple act of moving this far from big cities. But the habit of it was difficult to shake. She would find herself sketching Barry, a chair, a random arrangement on the kitchen table of a ketchup bottle, salt shaker, and dirty plate.

Today she had been drawing landscapes, mountainous ones. In the way they looked—distant uneven rows of teeth, peaks at odd intervals—they somehow reminded her of the tune Barry kept repeating on his xylophone.

The purest form of total random choice made mountains look as they did, the merest chance crisscross of volcanic thrust and gravity and the beating down of weather over centuries of time.

Only random choice could have brought Barry to pick out those five notes, and yet once he chose them, he remained with them as if, well, certainly, a randomness existed. It was all around them, in the way the veins in a leaf lay, unique to that leaf, never repeated in another. Each pebble on the beach was a bit different in size or contour or color or texture from every other pebble.

But the way Barry sounded those notes, it was almost as if in randomness there could be a message.

Jillian threw most of her sketches away in the cleanup process, but she saved one because it reminded her of something. She didn't remember what exactly. This particular mountain she had drawn was terribly tall and thin, needly and distorted like one of those desert spires formed when wind and sand have eaten away the softer tone to lay bare the core spout of harder lava that formed the ancient throat of a volcano.

Its sides were gashed by harsh grooves as it rose

out of a desolate landscape like a misshapen finger thrust accusingly into the eye of the sun.

Thunder rumbled nearby. Jillian shivered and ran outside to see if rain was coming. Clouds had begun gathering in the west, obscuring the weak sun with masses of leaden gray. Behind the clouds Jillian could see lightning at work. A major electrical storm was coming. But the flashes were strangely prolonged, as if frozen. Small distant points of light began skipping from cloud to cloud.

The air began to thicken with the sound of swarming bees. The clouds now seemed to be actually moving . . . down.

Yes, down and in toward her. Within them, strange flashes of colored light seemed to ricochet from one cloud to another.

"No," Jillian said in an undertone.

Across the rolling landscape, a kind of darker mass of cloud seemed to reach from the ground to the sky, a column that grew wider as it rose, almost like a . . . a tornado. Jillian felt defenseless, the way the girl Dorothy had felt in *The Wizard of Oz* as a giant tornado loomed on the Kansas horizon.

But this isn't Kansas Jillian told herself. And those bright-colored things dropping from cloud to cloud are not . . . not real? But of course they were real.

"No!" she shouted, suddenly frightened. Jillian eyed the safety of her house and turned slowly, very slowly taking the first of the long fifteen steps to the back door. She was terrified now and didn't want to make herself panic by running. She continued toward the house in a kind of crazed slow motion. Jillian entered the house and slowly and deliberately she shut the back door and locked it. She moved into the living room now and began lowering the blinds. As Jillian moved from room to room her movements unwillingly became faster. She went from a walk to a trot to a run, jerking the blinds down as panic took control of her hands and made her fumble and miss.

She stood still for a moment, trying to make sense of everything. That *had* been thunder, hadn't it? And lightning? That distant buzz, as of a swarm of bees, that had been something to do with the storm. And the clouds coming down toward her. But she'd never seen clouds do that before.

Barry was laughing. He'd never feared the violence of storms, for which Jillian decided she was probably grateful. But to hear the wholehearted way he laughed now, as the thunder clashed and the lightning flared, was a little too much for Jillian's peace of mind. No child had a right to be that happy.

She hurried into his room. He had stopped playing the xylophone and was standing at the only window in the house whose blind was still up. He was staring intently out at the sky and what he saw filled him with great glee.

He began running through the house, raising the blinds, swinging open doors and windows. "Barry, no!"

Jillian ran after him, shutting, closing, locking. They came upon each other in the living room. The boy had just sent the shade rattling up.

Jillian pushed the boy to one side and yanked the blind shut. As if on cue, an immense roar of thunder shook the house. Behind the blind a flash of lightning flared with such an orange intensity that it seemed to set the entire wall aflame. The buzzing roared around her.

Jillian cringed from it, but Barry clapped his hands and laughed. Now the house was dark. Only the booming flashes of firelight outside illuminated it from moment to moment. Jillian took Barry's hand and led him to her bedroom, where she picked up the telephone book and began searching for Roy Neary's number.

As she did, another clap of thunder and orange light bashed at the house like a giant fist. The television set went on. So did the stereo. Electric lamps began to switch off and on. She could hear, in the vastness of her storage closet, the distant sound of her vacuum cleaner starting up.

Barry broke away from her grasp, ran to the window and sent the blind skyward with one happy swoop. As he did, a strange stillness fell on the place. The television and stereo were quiet. The vacuum cleaner stopped. There was no sound at all, not even of wind or the distant buzz of insects.

Then Jillian heard it. It sounded like . . . claws.

On the roof. Scrambling across the shingles. Claws. Or talons. Long fingernails or toenails. Sharp, scurrying sounds.

She stared at the ceiling above her, eyes moving along in the direction of the scraping, scrambling noises. They stopped for a moment at the chimney.

And now they began to come down the chimney.

Jillian dashed into the living room and raced for the damper handle. At any cost, she had to shut the flue. Barry followed happily.

"Come in!" he shouted. "Come in!"

The clawlike sounds skittered down the inside of the chimney. Jillian dived at the damper, slammed it shut.

Instantly, a harsh roar of noise shook the house. Orange light flooded every corner of the room. All the window shades snapped up.

Jillian dropped to the floor, hands over her ears. The television was blaring away. On the stereo, the turntable was revolving. From the loudspeakers, Johnny Mathis was singing "Chances Are" in a huge voice like the growl of a lion.

Jillian ran for the telephone again, dragging Barry with her.

Eyes wide with fright now, she found Neary's number. As she held the telephone to her ear, instead of a dial tone, it gave forth the same five-note melody that Barry had been playing on his xylophone. Jillian jiggled the hook, got a tone like the angry *zzz* of bees, and dialed Neary's number. The room lights were doing strange things, dimming to a fitful smoky red, then flaring to a blue-white that hurt her eyes. The telephone was buzzing.

"Hello?" a woman asked.

"Roy?" Jillian's voice was a frightened croak.

"He's not here," Ronnie said matter-of-factly. "I'm his wife. Who's calling, please?"

The overload was so ferocious that even the air in the rooms seemed to burn orange-hot with a fearful buzzing noise. It was as if some giant high-tension tower, carrying thousands of volts, had toppled down on this house and charged it so thickly with power that—

The vacuum cleaner, like a prisoner being tortured in a cell, screamed in horror. The stereo speakers vibrated and burst apart.

A metal ashtray rose into the air and hovered for an instant, suspended in the terrifying heat of the air. She could hear the clattering on the roof again.

Jillian lost track of what was happening. The phone dropped from her hand. She slid to the floor. Barry was nowh—

"Barry!"

Racing into the room like an auto run amok, the vacuum cleaner began howling across the floor, chasing her as she jumped out of its way. It wheeled, charged again. Jillian ran.

In the horror of crashing, grinding noises and flashing, blinding lights, Jillian lost track of what was happening. Barry was—

"Barry!"

Somewhere in the distance she could hear over everything Barry's gleeful laughter. The kitchen. Jillian, beyond walking, started the endless crawl across the room to the kitchen.

The refrigerator was vibrating intensely. The door swung open, the light inside blinking on and off spastically.

Then she caught sight of her son. He, too, was crawling on the floor. Toward the dog-door opening. He reached it and started trying to wriggle through the narrow opening.

Jillian lunged forward and grabbed for Barry's foot. She caught it and started to haul him back in. She pulled hard. He slid across the linoleum toward her. The air smelled brassy and dank with electricity.

Then something pulled him away. Some force was tugging him outside the house.

"Let go of him!" she screamed.

Jillian gritted her teeth and pulled back. The boy's body shifted forward and back a few inches.

Jillian held on to her son until she felt, she knew, that if she did not let go, he would be dislocated. Sobbing, Jillian loosened her grip and Barry slipped away from her hands and out the little door.

In a flash, he was gone.

Jillian heaved herself up off the floor and threw open the kitchen door, staggering into the back yard, but Barry was nowhere in sight. She saw the tornado-like formation hovering above the house, as if parked, lit up by the tiny geodesic points of flashing and bursting lights.

Then the cloud eased away into the gathering darkness. And Jillian, not really knowing what she was doing, not really caring about anything anymore, started to follow, started to chase after it, until an immense shape loomed up, gigantic arms enfolding her. All the breath came out of Jillian. She fell to the stubble of a cornfield.

Cringing, she glanced at the giant figure entangling her. A straw-stuffed scarecrow looked down, smiling his idiot grin, arms flapping loosely as she slapped them away. Jillian had lost.

Barry was gone.

For a moment, Jillian lay there, sobbing in anger and pain. As she looked up through tears, she saw a lone star overhead change from white to blue to red.

And then disappear.

16

"What were you doing up on the garage roof?" Ronnie asked.

Neary had come in and gone straight to the bathroom to wash. "Some carpentry," he shouted past the noise of running water.

Ronnie went to the kitchen window and saw that he had knocked together some sort of platform at the peak of the garage, a platform on which a folding deck chair sat. "It's a lookout, isn't it?" she called.

She turned away from the window to find him with his face buried in a towel, scrubbing himself dry. "Roy, instead of building platforms . . ."

She let the idea drop. She didn't want to become the wife who nagged her unemployed husband into finding work. But she also didn't want to be the wife of the neighborhood fruitcake, sitting up there in his makeshift planetarium watching for orange Betty Crocker crescent rolls."

"You had a phone call," she said.

He dropped the towel. "Big storm toward Harper

Valley!" he announced. "You can see for miles up here!"

"She didn't give her name."

"She?"

"Or wouldn't." Ronnie took a small, measured breath. "Seemed kind of shattered to be talking to your wife."

"Who?"

"Hung up, finally, after a lot of thrashing-around noise."

Neary nodded absentmindedly, his glance going past Ronnie to the kitchen clock. "We don't have that much time. It's an hour's drive. Baby-sitter here yet?"

"She's here." Ronnie took another small, cautious breath. "Roy, I hope you understand that, after this, we can't be laying out money for baby-sitters. Not until . . ."

He had the good grace to look guilty. "I know. I appreciate your going along with this, Ronnie."

"But it's on one condition."

"Which is?"

"That when the meeting is over, you drop the whole thing. Isn't that why the Air Force announced this meeting?"

The fifty-mile drive went slowly, Neary realized, because Ronnie was not in a talkative mood. They approached the outskirts of DAX Air Base with about ten minutes to spare before the start of the meeting, whose time had been announced over radio and TV for several days now.

Up ahead the first sentry post loomed. Ronnie sank down in her seat. "I'll never forgive you," she said, "if we run into anybody we know here."

He stopped to ask the sentry for directions to the Civilian Information Center. "It's that big all-glass building," the corporal said, tucking a green visitor's pass in behind the windshield wiper. "You can't miss it."

"I sure can't," Neary commented. The building was huge, flat and thin, like a matchbook on end, acres of picture windows framed in anodized aluminum mullions. He parked next to someone's battered old farm pickup truck, another green card on its windshield.

The waiting room of this all-glass skyscraper was huge, endless. A civilian woman sat at a desk, took Neary's name, and gave him a name tag to wear, as she had the more than thirty people already sitting there.

"These people," Ronnie whispered in Neary's ear as they sat down. "They're all misled."

"Shssh."

"I knew it would be like this."

"You don't know what you're talking about," Neary whispered fiercely.

"Look at that one over by the elevators," Ronnie whispered back. She indicated a woman in her late fifties, raddled, white hair flying in several directions at once, her gaze as empty as an ancient headstone.

"Halfway over the edge," Ronnie murmured.

"On her way to the rocks below."

Just then, Jillian Guiler came through the door, and the reporters came to life, surrounding her instantly.

"Could you give us a statement, Mrs. Guiler?" a reporter asked as the hot lights were turned on her and the cameras started grinding.

Jillian, looking distraught and very tired, said nothing.

"Your report to the police was . . . ah . . . really quite breathtaking. We'd like to make the six o'clock. We lose our young audience at eleven."

Jillian seemed not to have heard.

Another journalist said to a colleague, "That's her, isn't it? That's the lady in the clouds."

"We understand no ransom note has been found."

The first reporter tried to follow up. "What about the FBI story? Is there any truth to that . . . that the child is missing? You gave the police a report. Would you mind repeating it for television?"

Jillian started to panic. The questions were furious, maligning, and irrational. Jillian was retreating to the elevators when she caught Neary's eye across the room. As the elevator arrived she formed the words. "They got him!"

"What?" Roy hadn't read her, but Ronnie sure did and buried her husband with one of her prize-winning rotten looks as the elevator doors opened and swallowed Jillian from view.

A master sergeant in full-dress uniform came into the room.

"Folks . . . you can go in now. Room 3655. Just follow me."

The Tolono group, lead by Neary and Ronnie, headed for the corridor. TV news cameras were waiting this time just on the other side of the doors. On went the quartz lights and the cameras started to whir.

Ronnie jerked her purse up to cover her face, just as if she had been arrested. "Damn you, Roy!" she muttered behind the bag.

The thirty or so civilian witnesses looked suddenly seedy, bleached out by the brilliant light from quartz bulbs in reflectors towering toward the ceiling of the room.

With the entrance of the Air Force team, and a phalanx of accompanying newspaper reporters and photographers, it became clear to Neary that whatever he had hoped to get from this meeting, what the Air Force wanted was publicity. So be it. For a change he and the military saw eye to eye. Let the whole world know what happened.

His initial feeling of satisfaction was dampened a bit when he saw that the Air Force spokesmen, all in civilian suits, would be sitting at ease on bent-plywood-and-foam-rubber contour swivel chairs, elevated on a platform a little above the rest of the room. In a hollow square around them ranged the voluntary witnesses, uncomfortable on folding chairs, unprepared for being the focus of so much publicity, still dressed for the most part in clothes they'd worn all day at work or on the farm.

"I'm Major Benchley," the younger man mused. "And this," he continued, holding up a large color blowup of an eerie high-resolution disc in blurred motion, "is a flying saucer."

That got everybody's attention, producing some "oohs" and "aahs" and ad-libbed responses to the effect that "I saw that one" and "That's the one."

"Made of pewter," Benchley went on after the stir had subsided. "Made in Japan. And thrown across the lawn by one of my children. I wanted to open up with this to show you that we're not all polished brass about these things and to make another point clear. Last year Americans took more than seven billion photographs, spending a record six point six billion on film equipment and processing. With all those clicking shutters, where is the indisputable photographic evidence that extraordinary phenomena exist in the skies over your homes?"

The "witnesses" seemed stunned or intimidated in silence until one of the journalists said, "How many times can we reach for our cameras when a sudden surprise catches us off guard? How many actual automobile or plane crashes are filmed and make the evening news?"

There were sounds of general agreement from the Tolono group, and one of the more rational of their number stood up and said, "To dismiss out of hand the evidence for UFOs will not quiet the fears that we may be living through the first stages of exploration from elsewhere."

"I am a reasonable person," said the little old lady with the remains of her photo album. "A reasonable person," she repeated reasonably enough. "All I know is that I saw something that was unlike anything I have ever seen before."

Nobody spoke for a while so Neary raised his hand.

"Let someone else speak," Ronnie hissed, reaching out to pull down his arm.

But Roy was already on his feet. "Look, sir. You people run the sky, right? Have you looked up recently? There's a whole airshow going on."

"I can only reiterate," the major said, "that after ten years with the Air Tactical Intelligence and the Office of Special Investigations there has been no indisputable proof of the physical existence of these things."

"Which things?" Neary asked.

Major Benchley had leaned over to confer with two colleagues. Now he straightened up and peered at Roy's name tag. "Please understand me, Mr. Neary. I'm not attacking your credibility . . ."

"That's okay. Just tell us what's going on."

"We're not sure. We can't just assume, as you seem to, that these were excursion vehicles from another planet."

"Well, it sure wasn't the Goodyear blimp," Neary said.

Many of the "witnesses" laughed. Ronnie did not.

"Let's say it's foreign technology," the major said in

a conciliatory tone. "Why assume it's *that* foreign?" He gestured with his thumb to the sky.

"Fine. Great," Neary responded. "Let's say the Russians are building and flying them. So what are they doing in Indiana airspace?"

That got a laugh from everyone—Air Force, civilians, press, and "witnesses."

Major Benchley waited for order and started over. "We have had some high-altitude refueling missions in the visible vicinity, and I'm told of a high build-up of static electricity—heat lightning. Also we have a condition called temperature inversion whereby a layer of cold air is sandwiched between layers of warm air."

Neary looked around the packed conference with mock incredulity. "You guys called this meeting to tell us what's going on and all we're getting are weather reports."

"What would you like to believe is going on?"

Ronnie tried to pull Roy down, but he took her hand away and said, "I'd like to believe the United States Air Force knows." Then he sat down.

"Who's going to pay for the damage to my land?"

Major Benchley blinked. "Pardon me?"

"I own the land where these people have been squatting at night," said the man, whom Roy recognized as the well-to-do gentleman he had noticed earlier. "This man over here"—he indicated Neary—"tore down several yards of my snow fence. There's trash all over the place from where these people have been staying up all night, eating Kentucky fried chicken and drinking beer. Who's going to pay for it all?"

Major Benchley pointed a finger at the landowner. "Did you see anything that night?"

The man laughed. "My family has owned that piece for more than eighty years and we've never seen one damn thing."

The television cameras had swung quickly to the landowner, and Neary realized that the meeting was starting to fall apart. If he didn't jump in fast, the focus would be lost forever.

"Wait a goddamn minute!" he said loudly, sensing Ronnie physically edge away from him as he jumped to his feet again. "I saw something." The cameras swiveled back to him. "This thing has cost me my job! That's how serious it is to me. It happened to me, it happened to some of you, and we want to know what it is!"

Benchley had begun talking over the last of Neary's words. "If the evidence is good, the case will stand up and the existence of extraordinary phenomena will have to be taken seriously."

"*We are the evidence!*" Roy shouted. "And we want to be taken seriously."

"Please, Mr. Neary."

"Please, Major Benchley," Neary mimicked him. "I would like to believe that I'm not going crazy. There are other people in this room who saw what I saw and they would like to believe that they are not going crazy. Is that such an unreasonable request?"

Major Benchley was silent for several moments and when he spoke again it was spontaneous. "I think there all sorts of things that would be great fun to believe in. Time travel and Santa Claus, for instance. You know, everybody, I wish I'd seen it. For years I've wanted to see one of those darn silly things hopping around in the sky, because I believe in life in the universe. Odds are against there not being life. The extraterrestrial hypothesis is merely one of many alternate possibles. We seem to want proof that out there is something that can solve our problems for us. It's an emotional situation we have here. We want answers too, not mysteries."

Neary sunk into his aluminum folding chair.

"Can you tell us . . . is your Air Force base conducting any tests in Tolono area? You know—secret testing, maybe?"

Major Benchley hesitated again and then, looking straight at Neary, said, "It sure would be easy to lie to you and say yes. You'd walk away with an answer you could live with. But this is not the case and I won't mislead you. To tell you the truth, I don't know what you saw."

Neary smiled, and then said, "You can't fool us by agreeing with us."

That produced a burst of laughter, which confused

Neary for a moment. He had meant what he said; it was not a joke.

Benchley laughed, too. Then he held up his hand for quiet, saying, "You must understand, all of you, that there are other considerations at work here. A certain hysteria sets in. We've had some schoolchildren burned quite seriously because they were playing with flares. Tonight we even heard from a lady in Harper Valley who blames this thing for the disappearance of her four-year-old son."

It was at this point that the old farmer decided to share his experience with everyone. "I saw Big Foot once," he announced. "It was up in the Sequoia National Park. The winter of nineteen fifty-one. It had a foot on him, thirty-seven inches, heel to toe. Made a sound I would not want to hear twice in my life."

"What about the little star of Bethlehem that led the three wise men to Jesus?" an addled lady with bluish hair and a Gideon bible asked. "This star has never been satisfactorily explained by astronomers."

The television cameramen were having a wonderful time.

"Sir, is there any truth at all to this Loch Ness monster crap?"

As they were heading through the lobby for the outside, Major Benchley came up to them, his right hand outstretched.

"Mr. Neary," he began. "I just want to say—"

"Why the hell did your helicopters blow up that

ridge without any warning the other night?" Roy shouted. "What the hell is that?"

"Roy?"

"Mr. Neary, I don't know what you're talking about. I just came over to—"

"I don't believe you!" Neary exploded. "I don't believe anything you say, Benchley."

Benchley, truly stunned by this outburst, backed off.

Ronnie pulled Neary away from the officer with both hands. "Roy," she said. "Stop it! Stop it!" She pushed him across the lobby in the general direction of a Coke machine, and went back to make their apologies to the Major.

Neary fed his coins into the machine and, Coke in hand, wandered off down a corridor, trying to cool off, trying to figure out what was the matter with him. He wasn't like that, blowing off at guys unprovoked. Benchley hadn't really done anything to him; the guy was just doing his job.

Roy caught himself staring at a small opening along one long wall. Still sipping away at his Coke, he swung open the panel door and there was a master control circuit box, an array of hundreds of circuit-breaker switches.

Neary's forefinger traced the office diagram for the building, which was tacked to the inside of the panel door. Then, moving quickly, he began snapping circuit breakers off here and there. His fingers flipped back and forth as he checked the diagram, threw another set of switches, consulted the diagram and flipped off more circuits.

"Roy!" Ronnie had found him.

Neary was smiling now. Shutting the panel door, he took Ronnie's arm and escorted her out of the building to the parking lot.

"Roy, what's the matter with you?"

"I'm fine. Everything's fine, just fine." He felt foolishly pleased with himself.

Neary started the engine and gunned the car out of the lot toward the sentry post. A line of cars was stopped there, drivers and passengers—civilian and military—standing by their cars, looking back toward the tall glass building. He braked to a stop at the end of the line, and he and Ronnie got out, too.

It had come out just right. He'd darkened some offices and turned the lights on in others. Across the entire broad face of the DAX Air Force Administration Facility, shining forth into the night for people to see for miles around, the windows spelled out three letters: U F O

The photographer and reporter looked at the week's worth of unwrapped newspapers strewn across the lawn, the bottles of spoiling milk in the delivery box, and then at each other. They continued up the walk to Jillian Guiler's house and rang the door bell.

They rang the bell for several minutes and knocked on the door several more. They tried peering through the drawn blinds and then went around to the back door and tried that. But they were unsuccessful. They were convinced that Jillian was somewhere inside the dark house. Their FBI and police sources had assured their editor that she was. But eventually they gave up and went away.

Inside, Jillian had boarded up every window. The living room was in chaos, as were the kitchen and her bedroom. Although she'd cleaned up the mess in the kitchen, the rest of the rooms were beyond her—even making the bed had become impossible—and the house remained much as it had been since the night Barry had been taken and the day after, when the police and the FBI men went through it and the fields and woods surrounding the house searching for clues.

She had taken all the phones in the house off their hooks. The police and the FBI had nothing to tell her; they'd had nothing to tell for the week that Barry had been gone. They said that if he'd been kidnapped, the kidnappers would have been in touch days ago. They didn't tell her what they thought had happened to Barry, but Jillian knew what they thought: that Barry had wandered away in the night, that he had fallen down or become frightened or lost something and was now out there in the woods somewhere, dead.

But Jillian knew that Barry was not wandering around lost, and she was sure he was not dead. She just had to wait and hope "they" would bring him back to her. And so she was waiting . . . and hoping . . . and praying. That was why she had locked the doors and boarded up the windows and taken the phones off their hooks. She didn't want to talk to any-one—police, FBI, press, neighbors, family, or cranks —millions and millions of cranks. She was waiting. For Barry. For a sign. For a signal.

To help her get through this waiting period, to help her keep her sanity, Jillian knew she had to paint. So she had set up her easel and her paints in a corner of the living room under a floor lamp—the light wasn't very good, but it would have to do—and for the past week she had been hard at it. Fourteen, fifteen, sixteen hours a day.

And always the same picture over and over again. A mountain, not a range of mountains, with valley and canyons, but just this one mountain. With harshly grained sides. With outcroppings of trees and brush. She must have painted twenty, no, thirty different but similar pictures by now. Jillian did not find her behav-ior obsessive. Not even unusual. She was going to keep on painting that mountain until she got it right— whatever that meant—or until she got a signal about Barry.

And so, Jillian Guiler listened to the men ringing the doorbell and pounding on the doors and scratch-ing at the windows, without really hearing anything. They would go away soon, they always did. And Jillian kept on painting the mountain.

17

It was near Huntsville, Texas, in an abandoned sheet-metal factory, that all hell was busting loose. The vast floor space was overcrowded with semi-trailer trucks and work crews speedily and efficiently loading them. The cargo was a strange collection of boxes, cartons, and crates. The smaller items arrived on conveyor belts; larger ones by fork lift. In one corner, men in stainless lab coats were packing metal canisters into Styrofoam-lined cases all marked *Special Handling*. A line of olive-drab jeeps waited on standby to trundle aboard. They bore no markings. Nor did the fiberglass modules that sat in the center of the square next to a thousand feet of unassembled spidery metal scaffolding.

A Volkswagen bus pulled into the warehouse, and Lacombe got out, followed by Laughlin and Robert. Aides rushed around behind and unloaded some simple Samsonite luggage.

"Is there anything Mr. Lacombe wants from his luggage?" an aide asked Laughlin. "We want to get it on the airplane just as quickly as possible." Lacombe understood most of the question and smiled a no thank you, continuing a tour of the mobilization all around him. Laughlin looked worried. After all, the Frenchman had been active without sleep for over thirty hours.

"I have excitement inside!" Lacombe told his interpreter. "Sleep will come when the excitement stops."   ,

Laughlin considered what little he already knew, and envisioned his employer awake for another ninety-six hours.

In another corner, away from the noisy activity, two dozen truckdrivers clustered around the dispatcher's desk. They were a motley group, some peeling off military uniforms and donning work-clothes and watch caps. The dispatcher was a no-nonsense lieutenant colonel with a very big stick. He used it to point at a mammoth map of the continental United States. The truckers pressed close and some chewed gum.

"You heavy cargo people are going straight in. Use the bypass routes marked on your interstate maps. The rest of you will receive alternate route assignments just as soon as we finish collecting information on weigh stations along your way. Now, we're staggering you Peterbuilts. We don't want you all coming in together. And I'm going to ask you two more things. Stay off the CBs and no unscheduled stopovers. If any of you have to 'go pottie,' well, you know what to do."

Above the din, a group of men stared at each other over coffee and cigarettes. They were in shirtsleeves and looked frazzled. Major Walsh circled the table and looked over the railing docks, the machinery, and all the noise. Walsh had never fancied home-front responsibility. This was his first year back from Special Forces Operations, both surface and clandestine, in Tanzania, Zaire, and Angola. And now, saddled with a security problem, Walsh was fighting mad that the team leader had drawn the line and not told him . . . everything. Walsh took a hit of coffee grounds and Chesterfield Long before kicking a wastepaper basket across the landing.

"You can't sell me an earthquake alert," he snarled, sucking his cigarette down to his fingertip. "There's never been such a thing. These are ranchers—sheep and cattle and Indians. They don't live in high-rise condominiums."

An exhausted-looking think-tanker wrung his hands out and bent back in his chair. "I still like the flash flood," he yawned.

"Where you gonna get the water, pal?" said someone else.

"We'll do a survey on dams and reservoirs in the watershed area. Tell 'em one's going to burst."

Major Walsh tucked in his shirt and tightened his Disneyland bicentennial souvenir belt.

"We don't have time for a survey. You people know that. You should know that by now."

Another guy, who had been attempting to break some sort of a record by contorting his Spidel Twist-o-Flex eleven times, coughed and interrupted.

"What about disease? You know, a plague epidemic?"

His buddy brightened at this and put down his pipe cleaning kit. "Anthrax," he bubbled. "Isn't there a lot of sheep up there in Wyoming?"

Major Wild Bill Walsh lit an Individuale and sat down.

"That's good," he exhaled. "But I'm worried it won't evacuate everyone. There's always a joker who thinks he's immune. I want something scary enough to clear three hundred square miles of every living Christian soul."

At the heart of the confusion below, Lacombe watched several workmen hoisting giant decals onto the bare silvery sides of the trailers. The decals read *Piggly-Wiggly Supermarkets*, *Coca-Cola*, *Kinney Shoes*, *Folger's Coffee*, and *Baskin-Robbins 31 Flavors*. Craving something sweet, the Frenchman popped a Listermint into his mouth and grinned at the American way of life. Then the steel doors opened, someone yelled "Westward Ho!" and the push was on.

18

"No, Mother," Ronnie was saying into the telephone, "I can handle it. But thanks anyway."

She had cradled the phone between her ear and her shoulder while she stood in front of the kitchen stove, stirring pots.

Ronnie turned partway around, covered the mouthpiece of the phone with her free hand, and said to Toby, "Go tell your father dinner's almost ready."

Toby hesitated and then just stood where he was in the kitchen doorway, watching and listening to his mother.

"You're not helping me, Mother. You're not helping. We have Master Charge till the end of the month. He hasn't seen a doctor. He hasn't seen anybody."

Ronnie turned and peered out the kitchen window. Roy was sitting in his patio chair on the platform he had built on top of the garage roof. The binoculars were jammed against his eyes as he slowly turned his head from side to side, sweeping the horizon.

"Yes, he's looking," she told her mother. "He's looking all the time, but not for work. I'm doing that . . . for me, Mother. Of course he loves us."

Ronnie nodded her head vigorously and then had to grab the phone to keep it from falling. She noticed Toby still standing in the doorway. "Toby, call your father for dinner . . . You're not helping me, Mother—"

The young boy moved slowly, almost unwillingly.

"Mother, I have to hang up now," Ronnie said, and promptly did so.

She could hear Toby's thin voice outside the house. It was almost as if he were afraid to raise it because he was worried about being overheard by the neighbors.

"Dad, Mom's got dinner ready."

Ronnie turned back to the window. Roy didn't seem to hear Toby calling. He didn't seem to hear anybody these days. Mrs. Harris from next door steered her car into the adjoining driveway and got out. Roy didn't hear that either, nor the disgusted plosive Mrs. Harris felt impelled to utter each time she found him on his lookout perch.

"Please, Dad," Toby whimpered.

His father let the binoculars drop to his lap. He stared down through the gathering dusk at his youngest son. Even through the kitchen window Ronnie could see that Roy's face was damp. He must have been crying behind the binoculars. She thought of going out there to him, but then decided against it, turning everything on the stove to a low flame.

After a while, Neary climbed down. He came into

the kitchen and stared at her for a moment. Ronnie saw that he'd dried his red-rimmed eyes. She also saw the prickly beginnings of a beard. Neary looked wiped out and, without a word, he moved past her into the family room on the way to the dining area.

Neary stopped at his miniature train layout, fixating on a little brown mountain built into the middle of the Lilliputian countryside. He picked up some shrubs and moved them to the top of the model mountain, which he'd reconstructed into a tall peak with deeply ridged sides. He felt his guts sicken as his brain drained him of every ounce of energy while working to make sense of the mountain image.

"It's not right," he said in a flat whisper, and left the room.

Since dinner was going to be delayed, Ronnie opened the refrigerator and put the bowl of salad back inside. The green bulb she had screwed into the socket turned all the food inside to unappetizing shades of gray-green. She made a face at the stuff. What had seemed a great idea just a couple of weeks ago now seemed trivial and silly in the face of her own husband's unreasonable state of mind. Ronnie closed the refrigerator door quickly.

When Neary showed up for dinner, he'd neither washed nor changed. Ronnie noticed that the children seemed to edge away from him. She always sat at the opposite end of the table from Roy, but now the children seemed to cluster nearer to her end than his, too uncomfortable with him to say anything.

She served and passed him his plate of salmon cro-
quettes, niblet corn, and mashed potatoes, with a
square of margarine melting in the center of the
mound. He stared down as if no one had ever told
him what to do with food on a plate.

Ronnie realized that the children were watching
Roy intently as he started moving the mashed potatoes around the plate with his fork. He molded the
potatoes into a little peak. "Not big enough," he said.
With a single back and forth motion he flicked the
croquette onto the tablecloth.

The children were stunned.

Neary reached halfway across the table and took
the serving bowl of mashed potatoes. He heaped a
gob onto his plate, shaping it into a large mound.
Neary froze to survey the situation. Not right! Another gob from the serving bowl. Not yet! So another,
and one more until the bowl had been cleaned. Then,
like a mad potter, Neary started to knead the white
mush with his hands into some kind of shape.

Ronnie was trying to catch her breath, and Neary
looked up at his family. They were frozen in place,
staring at him. Roy wanted to talk to them; he wanted
to touch them and make everything all right.

He forced a smile, then tried to make a funny face
about himself.

"By now you've noticed," he said, starting to laugh
at his own understatement, "something funny about
Dad. Don't worry, I'm still Dad."

Neary reached out to touch Sylvia, but she moved still farther away from him toward her mother.

He tried again, addressing all the children. "It's like when you know the music but you just don't remember the words? I don't know how to say it, what I'm thinking"—Neary pointed to the large mound of mashed potatoes—"but . . . this means something . . . this is important."

Roy looked up at Ronnie, who was concentrating on control. His mouth moved. "I'm all right," he was saying silently. "I'm all right." But no words came out.

Then Neary got to his feet and left the room.

The children's eyes swung back toward their mother.

Saddened, she said grimly, "Eat," and began forking the croquette into her mouth.

They all heard the shower start up, but they also heard over the running water the hacking, choking sounds of a man crying.

Ronnie stood up. "Stay here," she ordered the children, and left the room.

She listened at the bathroom door for a moment, then knocked twice, softly. "Sweetheart . . . Roy, please open the door."

There was no answer, just the terrible coughing sobs. Ronnie tried the door handle. It turned but the door was locked. She stood there, her hand on the knob. "Roy!" she called. Loudly this time. "Roy!"

He didn't respond; he probably couldn't hear her.

Ronnie made a decision. She ran into the kitchen and got a butter knife out of the utensil drawer. "Finish your dinner," she shouted to the kids as she headed back toward the bathroom.

Ronnie knew what to do. At one time or another, all the children had locked themselves in their bedroom or bathroom. She fitted the butter knife between the door and the frame and gently eased the lock open. Then she turned the knob and pushed the door. It swung in.

The bathroom was dark. Water was pouring into the sink and the bathtub was half full, water smashing down into it from the showerhead. Neary was huddled in the far corner of the darkness, his hands mashed over his mouth to keep the sobs inside. Ronnie turned off the sink faucets, but left the shower running.

Neary tried to smile at his wife. His convulsions subsided slowly. "It's like the hiccups," he said in a small, childish voice. "I started and I can't stop. What's happening to me?"

"All right, Roy," Ronnie said, holding herself together. "Mother gave me the name of this man. He's a doctor."

"I'm scared to death," he said, "and I don't know why."

Neary got up and sort of lunged over to the shower. He stuck his head under the spray. When he pulled out, Ronnie turned the faucets off and handed him a towel. She wanted to go over and hug his tears away, but she was too frightened. Another spasm of silent crying vibrated through Neary. After it passed, he opened the door of the medicine cabinet, somehow managed to get the lid of an aspirin bottle open, and, with trembling hands, got two pills out and into his mouth. Then he dropped the bottle into the sink. It smashed.

"Look," Ronnie said, trying to sound calm, reasonable. "What he does is family therapy. We all go. You're not singled out. And maybe it's not your fault anyway."

"I think maybe it's all a joke," Neary said brokenly. "Except look how I'm not laughing."

"Roy! Say you'll go see him. You've got to promise me," Ronnie told him, realizing that she was speaking to her husband in the same way that she dealt with her children when they were wrong. "Promise?"

Suddenly the bathroom door was thrown open the rest of the way and Brad hurtled into the room. "You crybaby!" he screamed at the image of his broken-down father. "Crybaby! Crybaby!"

Brad tore out of the bathroom and hurtled toward his own room. He slammed his door five times, wanting to smash it off its hinges.

"You know he doesn't mean that. It's only, for him you're always so strong."

Ronnie helped Roy into their bedroom. He had now stopped crying, but his trembling only intensified as he collapsed on their bed.

"I don't need a doctor," he told her. "I need you."

Ronnie had no idea how to deal with this. She beat on the bedspread with her small fists. "I can't help you," she cried. "I don't understand!"

"Neither do I."

"All this nonsense is turning this house upside down," she said, knowing this was no help at all.

"I'm scared," Neary said, grabbing her right hand.

Ronnie tried to pull her hand free, but he wouldn't let go.

"I hate you like this," she hissed as panic began to overtake her.

Roy reached out and pulled her down onto the bed.

"Hug me," he said. "That's all you have to do. Hold on to me . . . you can really help now."

Ronnie pushed herself away. "None of our friends call here anymore," she complained, not looking down at him. "You're out of work . . . you don't care! Roy, don't you understand, don't you see?" she cried out in a burst of panic. "You're wrecking us!"

Neary reached up again and folded his wife into his arms. His trembling seemed to pulsate right through, and Ronnie suddenly knew that she was really incapable of bearing up to all this.

"Oh, don't," she sobbed. "Oh, don't. Let me call someone. Oh, Roy . . . please don't."

But his fingers ripped at her clothing.

"I hate you, I hate you, hate you," she sobbed, hating what he was doing to her.

Neary gripped the blouse at her shoulders and

pulled. It ripped and the tattered ends pinned Ronnie's arms to her sides. He pulled the brassiere straps off her shoulders and slid the thing down her stomach, and then slid down to her breasts and—

Almost immediately his anxiety flowed out of him. He cocked his head to the side and stared down at her silhouetted breasts.

Ronnie started to tremble then, her teeth chattering, silent sobs racking her body. She was helpless and horrified, but Neary was getting something out of this for himself. Something constructive!

His mind raced on. No solution yet, but close. He could sense just how close. And, Jesus, he suddenly realized Ronnie had a beautiful body.

19

In Denver, the evening was cold and clear. The thin air whistled around the CB antenna of the immense semi-trailer as it started the long haul down the sloping highway to the north. It flashed by in the dusk, its gigantic trailer blazing red for a moment in the last rays of the setting sun. FOLGER'S COFFEE, the sign ran along its high aluminum flank.

The Piggly-Wiggly trucks, two of them, were already twenty miles east of Oakland and picking up speed on U.S. 580. Ahead lay Altamont Pass, over 2,000 feet high.

The sun wasn't as far down on the horizon behind them as it was in Denver. The drivers were hoping to make Tracy by dark and then to bore on through, filling the night with noise and diesel exhaust as they shoved their cargo toward the east.

It was dark by now on Interstate 80 running southeast out of Boise. The great semi, with its powerful diesel engine dragging the trailer along at sixty-five miles per hour, headed toward Hammett and Mountain Home, Idaho. The trailer bore the brightly lettered name and design of Kinney Shoes, but in the darkness the name was almost invisible, except when passing cars' headlights slanted by.

The trailer truck pulled in for refueling at a truck stop just east of Billings, Montana, where Interstate 90 ducks down through a corner of the Big Horn National Recreation Area. The two drivers would have liked to stop for coffee, but their schedule didn't permit it. They'd have to be through the Custer Battlefield monument and into Sheridan, Wyoming, by midnight.

The man pumping the diesel fuel looked up at the side of the truck. "Never saw that one before," he said.

The drivers and the gas jockey stared up at the lettering on the side of the trailer. TIDEWATER HOMES OF VIRGINIA.

"Kinda far from home, aren't ya?"

One driver wiggled his eyebrows. Of the two, he was the more communicative.

20

Neary hadn't really slept much at all. He'd kept Ronnie awake on and off. When he heard her breathing grow deeper, at about five in the morning, he eased himself out of bed and went into the family room.

Roy stared around the room with reddened eyes. He'd really wrecked the place during the last few days. Clippings from newspaper accounts of UFO sightings and the mysterious blackout were tacked here and there along the walls.

Neary groaned to himself and sat down in a chair, his elbow on the ping-pong table, where the model railroad layout—an island of neatness and order in his otherwise insane world—awaited him. The odd peak that Neary had built up, more like a caricature of a mountain now, loomed grotesquely over the tracks and little lakes and valleys, ungainly, menacing.

Neary stared at it and shook his head. "Not right," he muttered.

"Daddy?"

He turned to see his little daughter, Sylvia, eyes at half-mast with sleep. She had wandered out of her room, still trailing her favorite doll. The one that pees.

"Honey, it's so early," Roy said. "You should be asleep."

"Daddy, are you going to yell at us some more today?"

Neary gazed down into her clear, guileless eyes. That was how he looked to her—a yelling machine. And she was prepared to accept more yelling because she loved him.

Neary felt his insides turn over with remorse.

He leaned down and picked her up. "I'm okay now, sweetheart." Roy kissed his daughter on her forehead. He thought he might start crying again, but held himself together.

"Okay, Daddy."

He glanced miserably around the room.

"I'm finished with all of this. Swear to God. Finished."

Neary put the child back down and began pulling the clippings and photos down off the wall. "Look at me," he said, stuffing them in a wastebasket. "Watch me now."

Sylvia didn't know what he was talking about, but seemed happy that her father was happy.

Neary began tugging at the absurd mountain that he had built in the middle of the model railroad layout. He grabbed hold of the peculiar-looking peak and started yanking it. The mountain refused to budge, and Neary, using two hands now, wrenched the thing sideways.

Snap!

The top section broke off, leaving the mountain truncated, as if some earthquake had lopped off the peak, leaving a kind of plateau.

"Sylvia!" Neary shouted.

"Yes, Daddy?"

Roy's eyes were fixed on the strangely broken peak. "Sylvia," he cried. *"That's right!"*

It was no way for anybody to wake up.

Ronnie had slept late, utterly wiped out by the events of the previous night, by Roy's breakdown and by her own inability to be anything much more than a chest for him to cry on.

Now it was ten in the morning and what had wakened her was the high, shrill cackle of her children. She listened for a moment and realized that all her family was laughing. Roy, too. Groggily, Ronnie thought she saw a bush go past the bedroom window.

She struggled out from under the covers and threw on a robe, tying the belt as she moved out of the bedroom and into the ki—.

"Oh, my God," Ronnie gasped.

The family room window was wide open, the screen removed, a ladder placed outside against the wall. As she watched, a hydrangea bush came hurtling through the window in a spray of thick, black dirt. It fell onto a huge pile of . . . of other bushes, more dirt.

"Roy!"

Ronnie rushed to the kitchen door in time to see
Brad and Toby uproot an azalea bush and sling it to
their father, who ran up the ladder with the azalea
and shoved it through the window into the den.

"Stop it!" Ronnie cried.

"C'mon, men," Roy called to his sons. He seemed
happier than Ronnie could remember seeing him in
weeks, since the blackout.

Toby gave a cheer and began helping his father
throw dirt through the window.

"After this can we throw dirt in my room?" he asked
Roy.

"Stop it!" Ronnie cried. "Stop it!"

She came running outside, acutely aware that Mrs.
Harris was watching the whole thing from her second-
floor window. A neighbor across the street had paused
in the midst of mowing his grass and, transfixed like
a cement lawn statue, stood open-mouthed staring.
Ronnie knocked the dirt out of Toby's hands and
confronted her husband.

"If I don't do this," Neary said, still pitching dirt
through the window, "I *will* need a doctor."

"Do what? What are you doing?"

"Ronnie, I figured it out. Have you ever looked at
something one way and it looks crazy, then you look
from another way and it makes perfect sense?"

"No! Roy, you're scaring us!"

The force of Ronnie's statement did scare the children a little. Neary had been yanking at a geranium.

He looked up suddenly, as if seeing his wife for the first time. "Don't be scared, honey. I feel good. Everything's going to be all right."

He gave up on the geranium as his eye caught sight of a small aluminum patio table. Picking it up, Neary pitched it through the den window. It made almost no sound on landing, its impact cushioned by the layers of dirt and bushes on the floor inside.

"Don't tell me everything is going to be all right," Ronnie screamed after him, "while you're throwing the yard into the den."

Roy ran around to the front of the yard. Now he had his eye on two large green plastic trash cans that were standing at the end of the driveway. A sanitation truck was just pulling up and two garbage collectors were about to leap off the truck to empty Neary's cans. Roy accelerated and beat them to the cans, grabbing and emptying them on the sidewalk, then rushing back toward the house. He flew past Ronnie and the children, leaving two piles of garbage and two amazed garbage men in the driveway.

Moving like a high-hurdler, knees up, he hotfooted it back to the house, a container in each hand, throwing them through the window into the family room where they bounced off the patio table and rolled off the geranium balls and peat moss.

Suddenly, Roy was struck with a new thought. "Chicken wire," he said aloud.

Ronnie watched him hurdle the low ornamental fence that separated their driveway from the one next

door. A roll of chicken wire stood in the open doorway of the Harrises' garage. Mrs. Harris stuck her
head out the window as Neary picked up the roll of
wire and started to take it away.

"Whatever you're doing," Mrs. Harris said wildly,
"is against the law."

"He's putting it back, Mrs. Harris," Ronnie called
to her desperately.

She had gathered the two boys to her side, somehow communicating without words that the fine ma-
niac frenzy of helping their father was finished. Frightened now, Brad and Toby clung to Ronnie's robe,
watching the scene play out.

"I'll pay for it," Neary called up to Mrs. Harris.

"Take it! Take it!" Mrs. Harris brandished her hot
air blower at Roy like a revolver.

Now the baby, Sylvia, started to wail but Neary
didn't seem to hear. He tossed the roll of wire through
the window into the house and began foraging the
yard for more material. Ronnie, with all three children
clinging to her now, managed to get in his path.

"Roy, I'm taking the kids to my mother's house."
She was crying now.

Neary had been moving at top speed. Abruptly, his
forward motion was checked. He nearly pitched over
as he braked to a halt. "That's crazy," said the voice
of reason. "You're not dressed."

"That's what?" Ronnie shrieked. "You said what?"

Now it was her turn to move fast. Carrying Sylvia

and sweeping the boys along by the sheer force of personality, Ronnie hurried them all to the car.

"Wait!" Roy shouted, going after them.

She shoveled all the kids into the station wagon, then turned to him, saying, "I've done that." Ronnie rolled up all the windows and powerlocked the doors.

"Ronnie," he called to her through the safety glass. "Please stay here! Please be with me now."

"For what?" her voice sounding muffled. To Neary it seemed as though she were already fading away. "To see them take you away in a straitjacket?"

Roy started banging on the doors and windows of the wagon, Ronnie started the engine and jammed the car in reverse.

Neary stopped banging, but leaped on the hood of the car as Ronnie began backing it out of the driveway through the piles of leftover garbage. He could see his children's eyes widen with terror, watching their father pounding his fists on the hood and yelling. Then, as Ronnie backed faster down the driveway, he had to hold on to the radio antenna with one hand to keep from sliding off.

Ronnie hated this now. She wheeled back hard out of the driveway into the street, stopped abruptly, throwing Roy off the hood and onto the sidewalk, and then curled her toes around the accelerator pedal and blasted off down the street, around a corner and was gone.

Neary lay on the sidewalk in his filthy pajamas,

more stunned than hurt. Slowly, starting to hurt a little from his fall, he got to his feet. He looked up and
noticed for the first time that a half dozen of his
friends and neighbors had witnessed the whole thing
and were hanging in for a socko finish of some kind.
Neary wondered what they were expecting. Chimes?

"Morning!" he called to the crowd, waving at them
all.

Then Neary turned and strode magnificently off
along the grass to the window ladder. He stopped
to pick up the garden hose and turned on the water.
Then, trotting up the ladder with the hose, splashing
water on himself and everything else, he climbed
through the family room window, pulling the ladder
up and in after him.

Once inside, and with a majestic gesture, Roy
slammed down the window and pulled the drapes,
shutting out the neighbors and the entire outside
world.

In the family room, the show continued for quite a
while, fortunately out of anyone's sight but Neary's. He
worked steadily at it all day with nothing to eat or
drink and no human voice except the faint babble of
the television set in the corner, lisping its daytime
idiocies, blighted soap opera lives, shrieking game-
show contestants, banal junk movies.

It really hadn't mattered to Neary what the television was doing. Inside the family room something
much greater, something immense, was under way.
He had gotten to work like the trained engineer he

was, shaping out of the empty garbage containers and the lawn table a kind of rough core or support for what he was constructing.

Then, with Mrs. Harris's chicken wire, he had created a contour less rough, more complex, to the thing he was building. And then, making a muddy paste of the dirt, he had plastered the chicken wire until he had it right.

Still not content, he'd wet down newspapers and smoothed them over the mud to form a kind of hard-edged papier-mâché surface, stained with dirt, that uncannily resembled the surface of . . . what he was making.

"It's not right yet," he muttered unhappily around five in the afternoon.

He had built the thing from the floor up, braced it with uprooted bushes hidden inside the mud. It towered over him now, touching the ceiling nine feet overhead. Its sloping sides were striated in angry ridges. But he wasn't fully satisfied—not yet.

Neary caught sight of the landscaping on the model railroad. He snatched up miniature trees and shrubs. Holding them like chess pieces, he took his time figuring their proper placement. Just so. Here two pines. Exactly. And there a line of bushes. Precisely there.

"Right," he said at last. "Finally, it's right."

He'd barely had time to think of what he was doing —didn't remember, for instance, that he'd had three dry runs on this project, once a pile of shaving cream, once in the dirt of State 57 when little Barry had first sculptured this strange, conical peak, once with the entirely unsatisfactory mashed potatoes.

But he had it now. It could pass for the real thing, Neary told himself. Now that the mud had dried over the stiffening surface of newspapers, it really looked real, especially with the trees and shrubbery in place.

The fluted walls rose sharply to a kind of plateau at the top, a mesalike place. Around on one side lay a box canyon in which a peaceful Shangri-la Valley was shaded by more of the model railroad greenery.

Neary had been breathing hard all day. Now, as he stood there, slowly circling his creation, inspecting it for flaws and finding none, his breathing began to slow to a calm, peaceful tempo. He felt at ease now for the first time since he'd been seized by the need to . . . to *make this thing*.

He paused and squinted at the mesa top. Beyond it, through a window, he could see the normal life of the neighborhood outside. A car stopped and some people emerged, walked up to a neighbor's house and were greeted at the open front door. His other middle-class neighbors were mowing and pruning and watering. Cars moved by. Children played.

Neary shoved filthy fingers through his hair and stared hard at the mountain towering over him. He had made it. It had cost him, but he had made it. It was supposed to mean something, wasn't it?

But now that he'd sacrificed so much to it, there it stood. Meaning nothing.

"My God," Neary said out loud. "It's only me. Oh, my God, it's only me."

It was the low point of his life, and to make matters worse, the silly, plastic normality of the TV sitcoms now arrived.

Not really listening to them, Neary slumped down in an armchair, staring at the flat-topped pinnacle he had created and that had cost him so much.

He didn't actually watch the television as it ground through hours of reruns. He let it exist as a form of radio, giving him only the thin semihuman voices that trickled from its tiny speaker. Reruns.

Gomer Pyle was chewed out by his sergeant, not once but twice. Lucy got caught by her boss taking an extra hour for lunch. Rustlers invaded the Ponderosa, setting fires. On the stand the witness broke down under Perry Mason's questioning and confessed. Robert Young performed open-heart surgery in a power blackout.

About nine o'clock Neary stirred, went to the refrigerator and took out a beer. He popped it open. Surgery in a blackout, he thought. He blinked, put down the open can of beer and went to the telephone to dial a number.

"Let me talk to her," he said after a minute.

When Ronnie came on the line, he cleared his throat carefully. "Don't you think I'm worth it? Just don't hang up, Ronnie . . . Oh, please don't—"

Then he heard the click.

"Madge, tell me, how do you get your cakes so moist and fluffy?"

"Now I feel safe, safe, even with nervous perspiration."

Neary still wasn't watching the tube, but the flow of commercial pap had begun to filter more directly into his hearing. He was still examining the—what could he call it?—the mountain.

". . . crispy-good and just this much oil left in each one!"

Neary stirred and went to the telephone again. He dialed Ronnie's mother. "Put her on, please."

"Roy, I'm sorry, she doesn't want to talk to you."

"Put her on!" he shouted.

He waited. The line was still open. He held the phone in one hand and stared through the kitchen doorway into the family room.

He waited. No one came to the phone, neither Ronnie nor her mother. He strained to hear anything over the line, sounds of argument, anything, But it was still open. When he blew into the mouthpiece, he still got what phone technicians called "side tone."

So she hadn't hung up. So there was hope. The minutes went by. He eyed the kitchen clock. One minute to ten. As if it had been planned for that moment, he heard someone softly hang up the phone at Ronnie's mother's house. He cursed and redialed the number.

Busy signal. She'd taken it off the hook.

He picked up the beer and wandered back into the family room as the ten o'clock news came on. A man with the fashionably fluffed hair that hides his ears stared meaningfully into the lens of the camera, his eyes barely moving as he read the words off the Teleprompter screen.

"Good evening! Top of the news tonight . . . rail disaster!" To Neary the man seemed to bite off the words nourishing something in the announcer's soul.

"A chemical gas derailment," the man was saying, "has forced the widest area evacuation in the history of these controversial army-rail shipments. The remote area of Devil's Tower, Wyoming, is the scene of this latest mishap. Charles McDonnell is on the scene for a live report."

Neary's eyes began to glaze, but he continued to watch the TV screen. McDonnell, in a trenchcoat, stood with the mike in his hand. Behind him trucks were moving down a road while in the distance, mountain peaks stood against the sky.

"It's sundown here in the hot zone of Wyoming," McDonnell said, "and thousands of civilian refugees are fleeing the scene of disaster. Seven tank cars of the dangerous G-M nerve gas, destined for destruction by chemical means under safe conditions, overturned a few hours ago at Walkashi Needles Junction.

"There are no real towns or settlements in these wild Wyoming foothills," he went on, "but vacation camps and cottages are being evacuated now as army and marine trucks and helicopters comb an area one hundred miles in diameter that has as its center the peak known as Devil's Tower."

The camera pulled back to show the cortege of trucks moving past. Then, with a blink, the picture changed to a telephoto shot of a distant mountain peak.

"The steep sides of Devil's Tower," McDonnell was saying, "have made it a testing ground for mountain climbers from all over the world who—"

"Jesus!"

Neary was on his feet. In one jump he knelt before the television screen. There it was, the same mountain he had just finished making. There it was on the screen. There it was in his family room.

The same. The fluted sides. The flat mesa top. The trees, in the same positions. He stared at the screen, then at the model he had made, then back at the screen.

A huge grin split his face.

It had meant something. It hadn't been some sort of lunacy. He didn't know what it was all about yet, but he knew that the urge, the terrible compulsion to build, had a meaning. It wasn't the random insanity of a sick mind.

It was a message.

Forcing himself to slow down, he dialed the number correctly.

And got the same busy signal.

The smile left his face. He turned toward the den

and stared at the model he had created of Devil's Tower. It was a hell of a long way west of Indiana, he thought, a hell of a trip to take, alone and wondering.

Neary stared blankly at the open phone book. Idly, he flipped its pages. Then he began paging more carefully until he got to the listings for Harper Valley. Gold. Gowland. Guber. Guiler, J.

He dialed Jillian's home. Earlier, when he'd called to find out about Barry, all he'd gotten was a busy signal.

"I *am* sorry," a recorded voice told him this time. "Your call *cannot* go through as dialed. Please *hang* up and dial again. This *is* a recording. I *am* sorry. Your c—"

He dialed again and got the same recording.

It was going to be a long trip to take, but he'd have to do it alone.

Jillian Guiler had not left the house all these days. Except to lie down to sleep, use the bathroom, and eat an occasional, erratic snack, Jillian had not really left the living room or her paintings.

She did not look at all well. She had lost a lot of weight since Barry had been taken. More than that, though, Jillian had the look of someone who had suffered the greatest loss imaginable and was paying for it.

The corner of the living room where she had spent her days and nights resembled a deranged art gallery of heavily charcoaled and ruthlessly colored canvases of a mountain that had taken on many of the aspects of Roy Neary's mad creation.

Sometime during the past week, Jillian had turned on the television set, although she, too, hardly watched or listened. Now, however, her attention had been grabbed. By the evening news. She had tuned to a different station from Neary. Then by the magic of television Jillian got her first look at Devil's Tower.

"The army and National Guard units are supervising the evacuation. Dislocated families have been assured that the danger will have passed within seventy-two hours, once the toxin concentration is down to fifty parts per million. This means most residents will be back in their own homes by the weekend . . . of course, this is small consolation to livestock in the area, although ranchers have been notified that the quality of meat should remain unaffected. That means order that steak 'well-done,' Walter . . ."

A commercial came on and Jillian fell backward against her drawings. There was the tower again seen from the same angle as the television camera. The difference being that in her charcoal sketches there were no Huey helicopters perambulating the woodlands at the base of the gigantic peak. She stood rooted to the spot for so long that the network news ended and *The Hollywood Squares* began. Jillian picked herself up and took the pieces into the bathroom. Moving with small, deft gestures, like a repairman meticulously reassembling a watch, Jillian showered, did her hair, put on makeup, packed, and left the house. She prayed that she was on her way to Barry now.

A man who hasn't slept for a couple of days, Neary told himself, shouldn't have to go through all this. He felt shaky, but determined that the details of it were going to stay within his control.

He badly needed the car Ronnie had taken, but that couldn't be helped. Neither could the lack of sleep. He showered and shaved, which did help. But by eight in the morning, the false feeling of well-being had evaporated. He started walking to the center of town.

The situation, he told himself, is far from hopeless.

Neary had been carrying twenty dollars in his wallet. He had found another twenty Ronnie usually hid away at the back of the freezer where a burglar wouldn't look. Neary had also, with some pangs of guilt, looted Brad's piggy bank of four dollars and change.

By eight-thirty he was at the savings bank, drawing out forty of the forty-two seventeen on deposit there. By nine he was at the commercial bank, shoving across to the teller a check for a hundred dollars. After consulting the account balance, the teller shoved the check back to Neary.

"Sorry. Would you like to see our loan officer over th—?"

Neary tore the check to bits the size of confetti and

strode out of the bank. Damned bad luck. Then he saw the liquor store across the street. Hope! He flung the confetti into the air with a holiday gesture.

With that grudging combination of suspicious civility and terrible slowness that comes from not really wanting to do something, the liquor store manager nevertheless cashed the check. "You're running me out of twenties, Mr. Neary," was his only complaint.

The nine fifteen bus brought Neary to Cincinnati by eleven. He got to the airport in time to present the reservation clerk with his problem. She consulted two directories, three lists, and her supervisor before booking Neary on a through flight to Denver, a connection to Cheyenne, and a flight on a feeder airline with the improbable name of Coyote Airlines. She also reserved a rental car for Neary at his destination.

She seemed to be taking quite a while to do all this, but Neary didn't begin to get suspicious until he caught her glance moving past him to two guards standing a few feet to the rear.

Neary turned to face them. He could see they hadn't yet made up their minds if he'd "flunked the profile" or not. Like all airport security people, they had been trained to recognize several types of potential troublemakers by a "profile," which described them in physical terms: dressed a certain way, looking a certain way, talking a certain way. Neary could tell they were on the brink of fitting him into one of the pigeonholes labeled "potential hijacker" or "terrorist."

He turned back to the reservation clerk. "Miss," he said, "would you watch my things for a second? I'll be right back."

Picking up his overnight case, Neary headed for the nearest men's room. The two guards followed but didn't go in with him. Inside, he lathered his face with soap and water, took a quick shave, changed to a medium-blue shirt, knotted a dark brown tie in place and carefully combed his hair.

He walked out of the men's room and passed within a yard of the two security men. Only one of them recognized him. Their glance followed Neary all the way back to the counter, but neither guard made a move.

Padding the "profile," Neary mused, was easier than it looked.

The money part of it was easy, too. Neary learned that a shower, a shave, fresh clothes and a Master Charge card leave no one in doubt as to a man's solvency.

Now for the hard part. He got an envelope and some paper from the ticket clerk, bought a stamp at the insurance counter and sat down. He had no idea where to begin. He killed time by addressing the envelope to Brad, Toby, and Sylvia Neary. Their names looked strange. He'd never written them a letter in his life.

"Dear kids. I'll be away awhile. If I come ba—"

He blinked, scratched out the "if" and continued

writing. "When I come back I'll have some story to tell. I have to do this. I have to find out and this is the only way to do it."

His vision blurred. He found that his eyes had filled with tears. Brad had been right. He was a terrible crybaby. Neary glanced around, but no one was watching. He wiped his eyes and kept on writing.

"Boys, help your mother. You're good, reliable boys and—" He stopped. Helluva lot more reliable than your old man, he thought.

"I should be home real soon and—"

Not right to tell kids lies, Neary thought. He was disturbing them enough as it was. They probably hated him by now, or soon would. He had to make a better stab at explaining this. He owed them that much.

"None of this means much to you," he wrote. "Even less to your mother. But it's like the song Jiminy Cricket sings. Did I ever take you to *Pinocchio*? I can't remember if we—"

He rubbed his eyes. "Everybody has a secret wish. I can't explain it. All I can say is that it's stronger than anything else. When you wish upon a star."

The letter slipped off his knee and fell to the floor. Neary sat there, helpless, tears running down his cheeks. He stared bleakly at the letter as if it lay at the bottom of the sea, unreachable through miles of filmy, shifting currents.

Grunting with the effort, he bent down and picked up the letter. Without rereading it, he signed it "love,

Dad" and rammed it into the envelope. He got up and moved slowly, like an old man, like a deep-sea diver in a heavy leaden suit, to the mailbox.

He dropped the letter in the box and stood there for a long time, staring. U.S. MAIL U.S. MAIL USMAIL USMAIL.

When his flight was called over the loudspeakers, he was still standing there. The second time they announced boarding, Neary turned slowly from the mailbox. He straightened up a little. Then he marched off toward the waiting flight.

21

The Hertz Rent-A-Car station in this part of the world wasn't the usual sleek yellow-and-black office with a sleek young woman in her yellow-and-black uniform. In this part of Wyoming, the Hertz office was in Suggs' Garage and you had to look real hard to see the small yellow-and-black sign.

Apart from working on engines, Suggs hated every other part of running a garage. He hated pumping gas, fixing flats, replacing wiper blades and renting Hertz cars. And, to cap it off, he hated Roy Neary long before he ever had laid eyes on him.

"Oh, *you're* Neary," he said glowering. "You took your sweet goddamned time gettin' here."

"But you've got the jeep for me."

"I got *a* car," Suggs admitted grudgingly. "They ain't no more jeeps this necka th' woods, Neary. You're goddamned lucky I was able to hold onto that sucker back there. Christ, I coulda rented her twenty times over in the last day."

"People getting out of the area?" Neary asked.

"You gotta full tanka gas and that's the works. When you turn the sucker in, I won't be here. Just leave the keys in the goddamned ashtray."

Suggs was already out the garage door ahead of Neary. He jumped into the driver's seat of a Ford pickup and disappeared in a great cloud of dust before Neary had even taken the keys from the counter.

Neary took his overnight bag and a copy of the rental agreement around the back to see what kind of sucker he'd rented. "A Vega sucker!" he yelped, getting in and starting up the engine. He flipped on the radio.

". . . thousands of others are homeless," the announcer came in on cue. Obviously there was no other news in Wyoming but the evacuation story.

"The U.S. Army Matériel Command has issued these new restrictions. All roadways north of Crowheart on Interstate 25 . . . all roads leading into the Grand Tetons west of Meetestse . . . all multilane, undivided full-traffic interchange, gravel, local and historic stage roads north of Cody and east to Burlington, or west to Yellowstone Lake . . . all are now declared unsafe and included in the Red Zone. All are declared—"

Neary switched off the radio and examined the road map he had picked up in Suggs' Garage when Suggs wasn't looking. He located the newly forbidden roads and traced them back in the Tetons to Devil's Tower.

He sat for some time considering his alternate routes.

At Reliance, under a cloudless blue sky, the day was perfect for a picnic.

Instead it was roundup time, not of beef cattle but of evacuees. For miles now, Neary had been aware he was the only car moving west into the Tetons. The lanes east were jammed with over-crowded vehicles. He'd hoped to gas up in Reliance and keep moving, but for the first time, he ran head-on into the military.

A roadblock had been thrown across the highway right at the railroad station. National Guard soldiers, rifles slung across their backs, faces damp in the bright, hot sunlight, were herding people through what were normally feed and loading pens for cattle.

"Now boarding blue cards only," a sergeant roared over a bullhorn. "All evacuees with blue boarding cards move in quickly. Those with red cards form up behind the barricades. You'll be next."

He paused to clear his throat, hawk and spit without snapping off the bullhorn. The sounds echoed across the station area. "Stay in line. You'll all get aboard. Just stay in line. Blue cards boarding now . . ."

He watched a corporal fully six and a half feet tall take note of the Vega and start to lumber over, a stubborn set to his heavy jaw. But before he could reach Neary, a mixed herd started through the roadblock.

Steers intermingled with spring sheep, making progress almost impossible. The rich aroma of manure lay over the scene. "Git them woolly faggots outa my herd!" a steer rancher shouted.

"You leave them sheep be," the owner of the flock

warned him, "or there'll be beef by-products from here to Jackson Hole."

An Air Force chopper hovered over the milling cattle and managed to spook them into a mini stampede that cleared the roadblock. Then the helicopter lifted sharply, like a rising balloon, and headed at once for the high Tetons.

Neary was watching it disappear in the direction he longed to go when the shadow of the man-mountain corporal fell on him. "You got next uh kin in the red zone?" the soldier rumbled.

"Sue-Ellen, my baby sister," Neary replied.

"Last name?" the corporal pulled out a clipboard with a list of names.

"Hennersdorfer."

Slowly, moving the tip of a blunt finger like a snowplow down the sheets of names, the corporal made his way in and out of the *H* range of the alphabet. "No Hennersdorfer."

"My God, then she's still in there!" Neary exclaimed.

"We got everybody out by noon yesterday."

"Not Baby Sue-Ellen."

"No way," the implacable soldier told him. "Everybody's out. We made a house-to-house. Ain't no Baby Sue Nobody in there."

"I gotta check it myself," Neary said. "Ma and Pa'd never forgive me if Baby Sue-Ellen was killed because I was too lazy to go in and bring her out of th—"

"Hey," the corporal cut in. "You don't understand

English, do you? Everybody's outa there. Nobody's going in. And I got orders to shoot looters on sight. Get the message, Hennersdorfer?"

Neary grinned foolishly. "See you." He reversed the Vega and got out of there, but not before he heard the corporal talking with a buddy.

"Another scavenger, huh?" the buddy asked.

"Sweetheart," the corporal bragged, "I can smell 'em in a hurricane."

Neary's smile narrowed slightly as he left the area of the railroad station. He wasn't a scavenger or a looter, but if anybody'd asked him his real motive for being there, he'd have no respectable answer. "Researcher"? Or "curious person"? Maybe . . . "invited guest."

More like it. Because whatever had given him the lunatic drive and energy to mow down every part of his normal life and build that insane nine-foot-high model of Devil's Tower, whatever had induced him to do that was sending him a message plain and clear. And whatever else the message said, it was an invitation to Devil's Tower.

The only problem was how to get there, now that he was within fifty miles of the place. Walking, he'd get lost or shot. Besides, he wasn't all that sure he could successfully escape the G-M nerve gas. If that was fact. But at this late hour Neary couldn't decide who to believe. He was on his way to something important and blindly pushed on.

"Folks, I don't wish to alarm you," a man was saying as Neary parked his car.

The man was skinny, bald, with a long upper lip and a wide mouth, a talker's mouth. He had already collected a small crowd, but with the near-panic situation in Reliance, Wyoming, a crowd was the easiest thing in the world to collect.

"Let me tell you what you already know," the man went on. "G-M nerve gas is colorless and odorless. You won't have no idea in the wide world when you're breathing it or touching it. But then," he went on, warming to his speech, "when your eyes begin to di-a-late and your nose starts running, you're gonna ask yourself: 'Dear God, why didn't I buy myself one of them early warning systems the man told me about?' You're gonna wish you had."

About thirty people were clustered around him now. "And when that bloody discharge starts running from your nose and mouth," the man continued, "and your muscles seize up so's you embarrass yourself in your pants, you'll regret not taking this simple precaution, guaranteed!"

He held up a small cheap cage in which a dispirited yellow bird clung to a wooden dowel. "This here canary gives you precisely one hour of sure, safe, and certain early warning," he said, "and it's a godsend at fifty bucks."

Neary got out of his car and walked across the street to join the crowd around the bird peddler.

People were starting to shove money at him, which his wife took as he handed out caged canaries.

"Can't afford a canary?" he was asking in a high voice, his mouth working smoothly, easily as the words flowed, "then I got you a special on doves. They give you a forty-five-minute headstart, not as much as a canary, but then, they don't cost fifty bucks neither. Thirty dollars takes away a dove."

Neary pushed toward the stack of cages. "Let me have two canaries," he said.

"Two's better'n one. A dove's better'n nothing. And in the bargain basement I got chickens, twenty bucks a piece and they give you a whole half hour warning."

Neary fished in his pocket for money while with the other hand he reached across to take the two caged birds. Carrying them back to his car he was about to get in.

"Roy!"

He whirled around. "Roy!" the woman's voice called again. He stared at the crowd pushing aboard the rescue train. Surely the voice came from there, but—

"Roy!"

He saw her then, struggling against the flow of people, trying to make her way out of the crowd toward him. Jillian.

All the nightmarishness of the place seemed to focus down on the two of them. They fought to close the gap between them, but swarms of people kept them apart.

Soldiers yelled through bullhorns. Sheep shoved past. Cars kept trying to move down the crowded main street. The bird peddler's spiel was a cry of anguish.

The sun flooded the scene with painful intensity.

"Over here!" Neary called. Jillian was in danger and didn't realize it. The crowd had started to shove hard in its anxiety about getting into the train. Going against them, she risked being shoved to the ground, trampled.

"Get off!" he shouted. "Jump off the ramp!"

He waded through the crowd now, shoving people aside. Jillian fought her way sideways, then half jumped, half fell from the ramp.

Neary caught her. They held each other tightly as people streamed by on both sides, children, cattle, people carrying bird cages, an old woman with a tortoise-shell cat, a boy with a transistor radio glued to his ear, a man carrying two infants, a woman with four pillowcases crammed with possessions. The noise was frightening.

Jillian and Neary clung together, bodies pressed close. They were saying things they couldn't hear, babbling and laughing into each other's faces. Then Roy began to edge them sideways out of the crowd, through the line of steers moving along the sidewalk, and back to his car.

Jillian slumped down in the front seat and covered her eyes with her hand. Neary got behind the wheel and started the car. "Hold on to the canaries," he said as they moved off down the street. "What the hell, I don't think there is poison gas out there. Do you?"

"Roy," she moaned. "I'm so happy it's you."

"Me, too." He laughed.

"And your children? Your wife?"

This time Neary was silent. He had driven out of Reliance by now, part of a long line of eastbound cars. He pulled over to the side of the road at an intersection blocked by a jeep and two National Guardsmen.

"No turns here," one of them called. "Keep moving."

"Just taking a rest." Neary turned to Jillian. "They left me," he said then. "Ronnie and the kids took off. I was getting too flaky for them."

Jillian's mouth twisted sideways. "Flaky. That's what the FBI man told me. I could see he didn't believe what I was telling him."

Neary nodded. "Listen, Jillian, we didn't both come out to Wyoming just to turn around and go back."

"But they have the roads blocked."

"There's a way. This is a big country. This is beer commercial country."

She said nothing for a moment. Then she took his hand and brought it to her cheek. "I'm glad we met again."

Then Neary spotted what he was searching for all along. A stretch of countryside protected by barbed wire and not much else. The barbed wire had begun to rust in places. Neary backed up the Vega for a running start. He downshifted into hill-climbing gear for more torque. He rammed the gas pedal down to the floor. Under the hood the engine roared. Rear wheels spouted Wyoming dust.

The grille slammed head on into the fence. With a "bwoinng!" like a guitar string, the barbed wire snapped.

22

Now the Vega was careening across empty brushland. Tires popped up and down in potholes, woodchuck burrows, tiny valleys of erosion. Jillian had strapped herself in and was holding the canaries on her lap. Even so, she and the birds jounced up and down sickeningly.

"The police dragged the river for him," Jillian started again to get her mind off the air pockets. "I told them he wasn't in the river. He wasn't in the river! They went around to every house for five miles looking inside back yard refrigerators. Then they asked me if I had seen any strangers in the neighborhood. Oh, brother!"

Neary steered like a madman, whipping a wheel left and right to avoid the bigger chuckholes, half standing off the seat to see far enough ahead in this wasteland so that he could anticipate what was coming next.

There were no roads, not even cattle trails. All he could hope was that his tires and shock absorbers would hold out long enough for them to reach the base of Devil's Tower.

He could see it behind some intervening hills. He could see everything. As he glanced around, he could still see very faintly in the distance the long highway of cars heading east. He wondered if anyone who had seen him swerve out of line and ram the fence would take the trouble to report him to one of the many National Guardsmen along the route. He kind of doubted it.

In any event, here came something that seemed better than brushland. Neary tramped on the brakes, downshifted into low again, and rammed through another wire fence. The Vega shook its nose and dropped with a "thunk" onto a gravel road heading directly for Devil's Tower.

Neary slowed under the shade of a stunted scrub pine and inspected the birds. They appeared dazed, but Neary couldn't determine whether it was cross-country nerves or something worse.

He drove off along the gravel stage trail at a slower pace. It began to lead to higher ground now, skirting the base of foothills, rising constantly. As the Vega rounded another corner—

They both saw it at the same time. The Vega seemed to roll to a stop, all by itself.

They got out of the car and walked to the edge of the embankment to stare at it—Devil's Tower, looking a mile high.

"Good God," Jillian said.

"It's just I—" Neary stopped, moistened his lips. "Just like I imagined it would—" He stopped again, feeling that words could never express what he was feeling, the sense of *having got it right* at last, of having brought everything together so that, finally, it had begun to mean something.

The two of them stood silently before the awesome sight. Nothing nearby resembled this vision out of their dreams. The Tower stood alone, unique, something so one-of-a-kind that Neary felt a chill across his shoulders at the thought he had been able to reproduce it in sculpture without even knowing it existed.

He cleared his throat. "I guess we'd better move on," he said then, "or they'll spot us."

Jillian's glance seemed to click downward for an instant. "There," she said, pointing to a place ahead on the gravel road. "Isn't that a gas station?"

After a few minutes Neary steered the car into the abandoned station, really nothing more than a cabin that sold souvenirs and snacks, with a single gas pump out front. He lifted out the hose and shunted the cutoff lever. The pump growled. "Still got electricity," Neary muttered. He filled the Vega's tank and replaced the hose. "Eighteen bucks," he said under his breath.

"Roy." He heard what Jillian was warning him about, the faraway beat of helicopter rotors, moving closer. Neary pulled her out of the car and they stood in the doorway of the cabin, hoping the choppers would pass by without noticing them.

A squadron of transport Hueys cruising hazardously low zoomed over them. Flying somewhat higher than the rest were two flanking helicopters carrying clusters of chemical toilets from their undercarriage supports. Behind them a single Air Force Cheyenne hung protectively in the sky.

Abruptly, the Cheyenne shifted sideways and dropped like a plummet until it was just over the roof of the cabin. Before Neary could open the door and drag Jillian inside, one of the men in the copter, wearing goggles and some kind of breathing mask, pcked up a Polaroid camera and aimed it at Neary and Jillian.

Neary shrugged and produced a grin. The photographer seemed to be racking his special lens for a zoom close-up. Neary stepped out of the doorway and into the sunlight. He dug in his pocket and produced a twenty-dollar bill. Waving it at the helicopter, he walked over to the gas pump and laid the bill on top, weighing it down with a rock.

"Okay?" he called.

The only response was the pilot tapping the photographer on the arm. Then he sent the chopper ballooning into the sky. It headed off in the direction of Devil's Tower, where the other copters had already disappeared from view.

"That does it," Neary said. "Hop in."

He gunned the Vega up to seventy on the gravel road, taking the turns and twists on two wheels, ducking under tree cover whenever a helicopter appeared in the sky. At one point, waiting for a chopper to fly away, Neary saw a bird lying in the road, on its back, claws in the air. Silently, he pointed it out to Jillian.

"You want me to turn back?"

"What killed it, Roy?"

"Our canaries are still okay. I tell you, this whole G-M nerve gas thing is a put-on."

"Then let's keep going."

They sat in silence for a moment. Then both of them found handkerchiefs and tied them across the lower halves of their faces. Neary put the car in motion and they continued at a more prudent speed now that they were getting closer to the base of Devil's Tower.

He braked hard around a sharp bend, then had to stand on the pedal. Four olive-drab vans stood in a row, blocking the gravel trail. Neary shifted into reverse and craned his neck around to look out the rear window. As he started to back up, four more vans pulled in behind them.

Jillian and Neary rolled up their windows and locked the car doors without consulting each other. For a moment, nothing happened. Then the van doors opened and figures started coming out into the open sunlight. They looked like golden people.

It was impossible to tell whether they were military or not, but they were all dressed alike in sealed astronaut-type one-piece golden plastic suits with Plexiglas-bubble helmets and tanks strapped to their backs. They seemed to be hermetically sealed by the shiny metallic plastic. Neary thought they looked like a cooking-foil commercial.

One of them advanced cautiously until he was standing in front of the Vega. He then held up a small blackboard on which a message had been chalked:

"HOW DO YOU FEEL?"

The inanity of the question broke Neary's tension. He rolled down the window on his side. "Fine!" he yelled. "How do you clowns feel?"

The man in the gold suit put away the blackboard and gestured to them to get out of the car.

"The hell with that," Neary snapped. "The only gas in this area is from you guys farting around."

Another golden man with a Red Cross insignia on his right arm reached in and took the birdcage out of Jillian's hand. He walked to the front of the Vega and held it up for Neary to see. Both birds were lying on their backs, motionless.

Neary surrendered.

As soon as he and Jillian got out of the Vega, each was given a face mask and taken to a different van. "Hey!" Neary yelled as the van with Jillian moved off. But his followed an instant later.

Inside, the vans had been equipped as mobile medical centers. The men in the golden suits, Neary supposed, were in fact some sort of medics. It seemed to him, however, that they were functioning more as guards than doctors. He had no way of looking outside as the van jolted along rough terrain for some time.

When at last the trip was over and the medic-guard opened the van's rear door, Neary saw that the sun was starting to set. Its rays slanted sideways through a small campground of trailer offices, green tents, and vans like the one in which he'd been brought here.

In the distance, hard to make out in the gathering darkness, technicians were busy unloading the trailers of a great number of heavy semi-rigs. No time to witness more.

A golden medic helped him into one of the sealed coffin-sized trailers. Since the man was still wearing his bubble, he said nothing, nor did Neary. Time passed. Neary glanced at his watch. Seven P.M.

Suddenly the trailer doors swung open. Two masked men came in through the air lock. The man in the golden plastic suit immediately left. Neary had been sitting on the edge of an examining table. He stared at the tall, thin, gray-haired man, then at the younger man beside him as they removed their face masks.

"Well?" he asked. "You the boss honcho?"

The white-haired man frowned and turned to the other. *"Comment? Qu'est-ce que c'est un honcho?"*

The other man grinned. *"Le grand fromage,"* he responded. He turned back to Neary.

"We have very little time, Mr. Neary," he snapped. "This is Mr. Lacombe. We need answers from you that are expressly honest, direct, and to the point."

"So do I," Neary countered. "Where's Jillian?"

"Your friend is in no danger," Laughlin said.

Lacombe sat down across from Neary. His blue-green eyes seemed to crackle slightly with—Neary couldn't be sure—annoyance, amazement? Lacombe delivered a barrage of French with Laughlin translating merely syllables behind him. "Are you aware," he said, "of the danger you and your companion risked?"

Neary was confused by the French and the English. Whom should he speak to, the man with the authority or the man who was speaking English? "What danger?"

"There are toxins in the area," the two men told him.

"We're alive. I'm alive. I'm talking."

Laughlin continued translating rapidly. "If the wind had shifted to the south, we would not be having this conversation."

"There's nothing wrong with the air," Neary insisted doggedly.

The Frenchman ran his fingers through unruly gray hair. He pulled a pencil from inside his jacket and propped up a clipboard on the edge of a desk. "Some questions, Mr. Neary. Do you have any objections?"

"What kind of questions?"

Lacombe scanned the xeroxed sheet. Laughlin translated. "For example: Do you suffer from insomnia?"

"No."

"Headaches?"

"No."

"Have you ever been treated for a mental illness?"

"Not yet." Neary's weak laugh produced no response. "No."

"Anyone in your family so treated?"

"No."

Lacombe's pencil raced down the sheet of paper, making marks. "Bad dreams?"

"No."

"Have you recently had skin disorder?"

"No. Not unless—"

"Yes?" the Frenchman prompted.

"Sort of a one-sided sunburn. But I wasn't out in the sun."

The piercing blue-green eyes stared thoughtfully at him for a moment. Laughlin translated. "About the bad dreams. Do you wish to reconsider your answer?"

"No. Well—" Neary paused. "I had this *thing*. This, uh, thing in mind."

Lacombe waited, pencil poised. "More specific, please."

Neary shrugged. "It wasn't really much . . . just an idea."

The Frenchman frowned and checked his wristwatch. He ran his pencil down the list and picked up the next question. "Have you ever heard voices?"

"No voices. No little green men."

"Mr. Neary," Lacombe began carefully, slowly, "have you ever had a close encounter? A close encounter with something very unusual?"

That one clicked and Neary started a sloppy smile, "Who are you guys?" He searched them for a few specific truths. They had his candy. But this wasn't fair play, only one piece at a time.

Lacombe looked up and offered another piece. "Ever hear a ringing in the ears?" Laughlin interpreted. "An almost agreeable, sometimes pleasant, ringing. A particularly melodic tone or series of tones?"

"Who are you people?" Neary insisted.

Lacombe spoke in whispers to Laughlin. They were exchanging notes in French, and Neary just sat there on his stool, feeling complete isolation.

"Is that it?" Neary cried. "Is that all you're going to ask me?" The frustration of these absurd weeks surged out of him. "Well . . . I got a couple of thousand goddamn questions! Are you the head man around here? I want to lodge a complaint. You have no right to make people crazy! You think I personally investigate every news story on Walter Cronkite? If this is just a cloud of gas . . . why is it I know this mountain in every detail, and I've never been here?"

Neary had spoken the magic words and now it was Lacombe who "clicked."

The Frenchman stopped and studied this strange American. There was a knock on the door. Bad timing.

Another golden man—without medical insignia—stepped inside.

"Com-Sec says to take them to Evac-Reliance and a bus ride home," the bubble-headed fellow said.

The man backed out of the room.

Lacombe returned to his seat and motioned to Neary and Laughlin to do the same. Now Lacombe was quite excited. "You tell me," he said in slow, careful English, "you imagined this mountain before you had discovered its existence? It manifested itself to you in many ways. Shadows on the wall, ideas, geometric images that to you, Mr. Neary, seemed like progress toward the familiar but sadly and for so long without any meaning until, finally, it came to you. And it was right!!"

Neary held back his tears with great effort. He nodded bleakly.

"And you feel—" Lacombe paused, obviously searching for just the right word. He found it. "*Compelled* to be here?"

"I guess you might say that," Roy responded out of the depth of irony he had never known he possessed.

Ignoring that, Lacombe took an envelope from David Laughlin, opened it and produced a dozen colored Polaroids which he handed to Neary.

"These people? These are all people who were trying to get to the mountain. They are strangers to you?"

Roy went through the stack. "Yes," he said. "All except her." He held up Jillian's picture.

Lacombe took all the pictures back, put them in the envelope and gave it back to Laughlin.

"By being here," the Frenchman asked quietly, "what do you expect to find?"

Neary struggled to formulate a reply. What the hell *was* he doing here? "The answer," he said, at last. "That's not crazy, is it?"

Lacombe got up to go. "No, Mr. Neary, it is not." When he reached the door he turned back quickly, spoke simply. "I want to say to you that you are not alone. I wish you could know this. You have many friends and . . . I envy you."

The three men paused in the air lock to put their helmets on. On a long wall table lay five or six unused masks, some long rubber gloves and a cheap birdcage. In it were two canaries. They huddled together in a corner and watched Neary's movements with too-bright eyes. Laughlin opened the outer door of the air lock and the three men walked into the early evening.

The sky in the west still glowed red, but overhead the heavens had darkened to a deep velevty blue. Neary glanced up and saw stars coming out in clusters through the thin mountain air.

Lacombe and his interpreter walked him to a Huey assault chopper, its engines purring but its rotor still.

"No!" Neary exclaimed. "I'm not going back. I'm not going on any bus ride home!"

A gloved hand slid open the starboard door. Neary could see seven or eight civilians, all wearing masks, seated inside. Jillian lifted her hand listlessly, as if she had no energy left. Neary climbed aboard. One of the copter pilots handed a packet to Laughlin, standing on the ground below.

Laughlin leafed through the packet of paper and cardboard. He passed it along to Lacombe. "You see? Everyone drew his own version of the Tower before they came here."

The Frenchman studied the drawings, some no more than doodles, some carefully done in crayon or felt-tipped pen. After a long moment he looked up through the open door of the Huey and stared at the people inside. Then his sharp glance shifted to the pilot and he spoke quickly to Laughlin in French.

"You are not to take off," Laughlin relayed to the pilots.

"Sir, I have my orders from Com-Sec."

"You have my orders now. No departure."

"Sorry, sir," the pilot said in a mulish tone. There was something about the "sorry" that conveyed its opposite and something about the "sir" that downgraded it to an epithet.

""Five minutes, then!" Lacombe snapped.

The pilot relented and held up three fingers.

Lacombe and Laughlin were off and running toward an OD trailer a hundred yards closer to the Devil's Tower.

23

The communications trailer was darkened at one end
to allow the radar officers to watch their scopes. At
the other end, where a window looked out at the
waiting helicopter in the distance, two civilians—
Lacombe and his translator—squared off with a project security officer known to them as Wild Bill.

Wild Bill was about Lacombe's age, Dave Laughlin
estimated, somewhere near fifty—or at least looking
that age, regardless of how old he really was. Wild
Bill was short, squat, and loud. He had a flat, monoto-
nous drawl, as if face-to-face conversation between
human beings was of the same order of verbal traffic.
Similar to control tower and approaching aircraft, or
NASA Mission Control and project astronauts.

"*You* cannot send them away!" Lacombe burst out,
more agitated than his interpreter had ever seen him.
"I will take responsibility for keeping them here."

"You have no responsibility this side of 'Mayflower,'" Wild Bill responded almost mechanically.
"As Com-Sec, I have all the base camp responsibility."

"Major Walsh," the Frenchman began.

Wild Bill interrupted. "Three miles from right here, you are the boss. Christ, we've spent enough setting up the D.S.M. It's taken us ten zillion dollars. That's your bailiwick. This down here is mine."

"You don't understand," Laughlin said, trying to break up the irreversible conflict shaping between the two men. "Whatever you're doing down here at the base camp is for only one reason, so Mr. Lacombe's project can proceed on schedule upstairs."

"I appreciate that." Wild Bill's eyes, each neatly imbedded in a tight half-moon of suety flesh, almost closed shut as he grimaced. "But you people have to understand how military discipline works."

"I don't want those people removed," the Frenchman repeated.

Wild Bill took a long, steadying breath. "We have a chain of command three weeks long," the major went on. "This incursion into base camp . . . How do we know these aren't saboteurs, fanatics or cultists on a negative errand. That's the only way our chain of command is set up to handle an incursion. It's too late to handle it any other way."

"This is a small group of people," Lacombe· said, speaking very slowly and turning now and then for a helping word from Laughlin, who was magnificent, supplying the emotional and linguistic equivalents when Lacombe's excitement forced him to shift to his native tongue. He gestured out the window at the waiting helicopter. "They share a common vision. It is

a mystery to them and to me why they felt compelled
to come here."

Wild Bill hunched his meaty shoulders in a bull-
like shrug. "You want to go over my head for clear-
ance, you'll have to copter out the message because
we've got communications blacked out down here
to the point where even I don't know what's going
on."

The Frenchman shoved a handful of drawings at
the major. "Why were these not shown to me until
the last moment?"

Wild Bill took the bits of paper and spread them
out on the table. "Interesting," he mused.

"We know very little about these people," Lacombe
told him. "Just the answers to our questionnaire. But
who are they? *Why* did they all draw these pictures?
Why were they compelled to come here when they
saw Devil's Tower on television?"

The tubby man shrugged. "Got to be coincidence."
Obviously unhappy with the idea, he continued
pushing around the drawings with one pudgy finger.
"These are just a random assortment of people," he
said then. "Nothing special about them. This guy
Neary you talked to. He's Mr. Joe College. The woman
with him says she's looking for her little boy. Who
knows?"

"What about this one?" Lacombe demanded, pointing to a larger drawing in some detail. The major
turned it over and read the name of the artist on the
back. "Larry Butler. We checked him out. He's from

Los Angeles. Sells real estate. Used to be a bit player in Western flicks. He's another nobody."

"This one?" the Frenchman wanted to know.

Wild Bill stared at the scrawled crayon sketch. "A Mrs. Rosen from Kansas City. She's a grandmother. Her husband is with her. Retired. On vacation. We ran checks on all these people, direct to Washington. They're nobodies. A few traffic violations. No criminal records."

"And this one?"

"George Fender. Garagé mechanic, Fort Worth, Texas. World War Two Veteran. Wounded on Guadalcanal."

"This one?"

"We don't have this kind of time," the major said. "Take my word for it. These folks are nothing."

"This one?" Lacombe insisted.

"Elaine Connelly. Schoolteacher. Bethesda, Maryland. Widow. Married son, three grandchildren." Wild Bill gave a snort of exasperation. "I suppose you want a rundown on the other two?"

"Of course!" Lacombe responded.

"Mr. and Mrs. Arthur Penderecki, Hamtramck, Michigan. He's a meat cutter. She's a secretary. They're on their honeymoon. She teaches Sunday School." He took a sharp breath. "Enough!" he snapped then.

"But there is no connection," the Frenchman said.

"I don't care whether there is or there isn't. My

responsibility is to ship the lot of them off the premises. Now!"

"But you have said it yourself. They are not harmful people. They are nobody in particular."

"That's how they *seem*," the major reminded him. "On a quick five-minute check, that's all we've uncovered."

"Nine people who had the same vision."

"So you say."

"Who have the same compulsion to come here."

"We're wasting time," Wild Bill said in a controlled yelp. "It's not my time. It's your time. You're the man with the deadline. But once you make it my deadline, that's it. We move. Now!"

Lacombe said nothing for a long moment. His gray-haired head had reared back on his neck during this confrontation. Now it relaxed slightly. "I must find out what is the meaning of these people's compulsion. Why they had to come here. Maybe—"

"No way," Wild Bill snapped.

"*Écoutez-moi!*" Lacombe snarled angrily. "For every one of these people there must be thousands out there also touched by this implanted vision."

"It's just a coincidence," the major suggested.

"It is a sociological event," the Frenchman corrected him, "of surprising importance. The answer to why they've come is perhaps the most important information we will have developed in the project's entire existence."

"'I'm terminating this conversation.'"

Lacombe's arm reached out. His fingers grabbed the front of Wild Bill's combat jacket. "You will listen to me, Major Walsh."

Wild Bill's tiny eyes widened. Nobody had grabbed the front of his jacket since he'd been a lieutenant fresh from the Point.

"You're gonna be late upstairs at the D.S.M." he told the Frenchman.

"Écoutez-moi, tête-de-merde."

Wild Bill turned to Laughlin. "Wha'd he say?"

24

Inside the big Huey helicopter, Neary, Jillian and the other civilians who had "incursed" the base camp sat quietly, almost numbly, gas masks fastened, only their eyes moving this way and that as they tried to understand what had happened to them.

What was going to happen now, Neary told himself, was obvious. They'd be lifted out in another few minutes and that would be the end of the whole wild thing. He'd never learn what the mountain meant. Jillian would never find Barry. None of these people would ever know anything.

And all because the base camp's strategy for keeping out visitors was hard to beat. The advertised nerve gas danger could be real. It would be like the military, he mused, to actually let a few whiffs of it into the area and knock off enough wildlife to convince the skeptics, or were the wildlife only stunned? Neary remembered the two canaries in the cheap metal cage sitting inside the air lock of one of the

trailers. Whose canaries? His? But he'd been shown
his canaries were dead. If not dead—

He was sitting next to Jillian, their thighs pressed
against each other, her eyes closed. She'd come a long,
long way, Neary thought, and for nothing. They had
all killed themselves to get here. And now it was going
to be over before it even began.

He got to his feet. The seven other civilians glanced
at him. Jillian's eyes opened and she looked up at
him.

Slowly, moving with great precision, Neary unfas-
tened his gas mask. The snaps made noises like rifle
shots. He ripped off the mask and threw it to the
ground. If this was the bravest thing he'd done, it
was also, all of a sudden, the easiest. It made the
most sense, too.

He took in a long deep breath.

The others looked horrified. Then, so fast he almost missed the movement, Jillian tore the mask from
her face. She stood up beside Neary and took a full
breath.

"You'll be poisoned," a little seventy-year-old man
told him.

"Mister," Neary told him, "there is nothing wrong
with this air. The military just doesn't want any witnesses here."

A little old lady, perhaps the little old man's wife,
said quiveringly, "But if the army doesn't want us
here, this isn't our business."

"We only wanted to see the mountain," the old man

said apologetically to Neary. "It was such a coincidence when I painted it. No one bothered to tell us about the air."

"How did you locate this spot?" Jillian asked him.

"No problem. I looked it up in *Famous Mountains of the Western Hemisphere*. Did you know that President Theodore Roosevelt proclaimed this our country's first national monument on September 24, 19. . . ."

A fellow in his forties stood up and ripped off his helmet. He had a suntan, longish hair and acted like a guy with a lot of money. He took a deep breath, exhaled and then said, "Oh, Christ! It's better than the air in Los Angeles."

Two others—a man and a woman—stood up and with nervous, trembling fingers, took off their helmets. Their faces were drawn and thin, and they had the look of people on the downside of physical exhaustion, people who had probably been socially criticized for months. They looked scooped out from the inside, and they were unable to face Neary or the others.

But Roy turned to face all his companions. He spoke loudly above the idling rotors. "Who's for staying?" he asked.

Jillian raised her hand. Then the fellow from Los Angeles. Finally, the old couple. Everyone else looked away.

"Okay," Neary said. "You'll have to keep up with me and run very fast."

At that moment, the helicopter door started sliding shut behind him. Roy desperately used his arm as a door jamb. The guard outside opened the door to see what was going on and saw a bunch of the detainees with their helmets off. As he was registering this, the fellow from Los Angeles rushed to Neary's side.

"Now!" Roy shouted. *"Run for the mountain!"*

They pushed the door halfway open and Neary struck out and hit the guard in the neck, just under the helmet, with his foot. Roy, Jillian, and the Los Angeles man vaulted awkwardly over the fallen soldier and headed for the tree line.

To each side of them were Piggly-Wiggly and Baskin-Robbins trucks where technicians—without helmets and body protection—were unloading electronic equipment and a lot of crates labeled *Lockheed* and *Rockwell—Special Handling* flashed by their eyes as they raced away.

The other detainees, including the old couple, who decided to run for it were stopped by the other guards within two steps of the helicopter door. Neary was running with every fiber of strength and glanced up at the mountain that had haunted their dreams. Now they would get the chance to unravel the nightmare.

Back in the communications trailer, Lacombe, utterly frustrated by Wild Bill's ignorance and intransigence, said in failing English, "You do not understand!" Then, in rapid-fire French: "The mountain was the key. And the gift in the Mexican desert was a clue. For us, to open our minds and let them in."

Laughlin finished translating, and then Lacombe

had a new thought. He translated it himself from the French. *"They were invited!"* he shouted. *"They were invited!"*

None of this sank in. Laughlin could see that.

But something outside the window caught Lacombe's eye. He drifted over and watched the three detainees heading for the trees. He didn't say anything, but a slow smile spread over his face.

Moving in the shadows of dusk, Neary led his two companions around a helicopter pad and into the brushlands at the base of the mountain. He fell to the ground to catch his breath and to give the others a chance to catch up with him. When they did, Roy started taking off his space suit and motioned to them to do the same.

He stuck out his ungloved hand. "Hiya. Name's Roy."

"Larry Butler."

Still puffing hard, Neary said, "We can't stay here. Go on to the tree line and wait for me there."

Larry and Jillian took off immediately. Roy took another moment to catch his breath, looking down at the activities at the base camp and then he, too, started running hard up the mountain toward the tree line, two hundred yards away.

A moaning siren howled in the darkness. Searchlights began to crisscross the landing pad. The door to the communications trailer burst open, and a guard, gasping for breath inside his helmet, stumbled in.

"Overpowered me, sir!"

"How many?" Wild Bill barked.

"Three. Three of them, sir. We got the rest."

Wild Bill grabbed a pair of binoculars off the table, glared darkly at Lacombe and Laughlin and strode fast out of the trailer. The others followed.

In the background, three helicopters were already rising vertically, testing their powerful quartz-iodide searchlights. About a dozen Special Forces soldiers in regular gear, including gas masks strapped to their belts, were loading their rifles. They were carrying semiautomatic M-14s with infrared sniper sights.

Wild Bill swept the tree line with his binoculars. They had set up an improvised field headquarters near the helicopter pads. The Major and Lacombe were on two field phones.

"I'll have them off the mountain in one hour," Wild Bill shouted into his phone.

A voice responded on their phones. "Do a photometric analysis of the northern face. Use infrared."

"It's already ordered."

"If they are not off the mountain by 0800 hours, dust the northern face with E-Z Four. Get back to me."

"What is . . . E-Z Four?" Lacombe asked, alarmed.

"A sleep aerosol," Wild Bill told him on the telephone, although they were standing two feet apart. "Same stuff we've been using on the livestock decoys. It's fast-acting, extremely local, and should detoxify in several hours. They'll be out cold for six hours and wake up with one hell of a headache."

In careful English, the Frenchman spoke into his

phone. "We do not choose this place. We do not choose this time. We do not choose these people. To stop them is not for us to choose."

"This was a perfect strategic vacuum until he siphoned air into it," Wild Bill told the phone.

"They belong here more than we," Lacombe said sadly.

Through the fir trees, the top of Devil's Tower stood out against the evening sky. It appeared insurmountable to the three escapees as they trudged wearily up a steep incline, slipping in the loose topsoil and pine needles.

Jillian stumbled and fell, sliding backward, downward, before catching hold of some undergrowth. Larry Butler also fell, but was up in a moment. Roy stopped, waiting for them to catch up to him. Then he heard the by-now-familiar noise above him.

Suddenly three helicopters lit up the uppermost region of the mountaintop way ahead of them and started maneuvering around the partially hidden areas, stabbing away at them with their brilliant searchlights.

"They've given us a lot of credit," Larry said, breathing heavily. "That's a good two hours on foot."

"Do you see that notch in the mountain?" Neary asked, pointing through the darkness.

There was, in fact, a narrow passage through to the other side.

"We can probably make that in no time," he said,

trying to cheer himself up, as well as Jillian and Larry.

Butler got set to make the dash. "I should've never given up jogging," he said, grinning.

A formation of red and green helicopter lights hovered above the plateau and then disappeared as the choppers started to sweep the far side of the mountain.

"There go four more," Jillian counted. "There's another ravine that leads up the hill," she said hesitantly. "I remember it from my painting . . . It's an easier climb. It starts on the northeast face and—"

"That's no good," Neary said definitively. "It falls off at the top three hundred feet straight down. We'd have to be experienced climbers. This way, it's a gradual roll to the other side."

"What do you think is on the other side?" Butler asked.

"There's a box canyon. It's rimmed with trees and hiking trails."

Jillian looked at Neary. "I never imagined that," she said. "I just colored the one side."

"There was no canyon in my doodles," Larry agreed.

"Next time," Neary said, "try sculpture."

Back at the bivouac area, near the helicopter pad, a group of army engineers was relaying ten gallon stainless-steel canisters of E-Z Four to the waiting helicopters. The men worked in silence beneath the howling rotors and handled the stuff as though it might spill out at any moment and fell them all.

Wild Bill stood off to the side, watching the operation. He checked his watch and looked up the mountain. He knew the platoon of Special Forces troops had fanned out and were moving steadily up the mountain.

An aide handed Wild Bill a field phone.

"Pyramid to Bahama."

"Bahama," Wild Bill answered. "Go ahead."

"Nothing to report from midstation. Once they reach the shoulder there's a thousand places for concealment. I'd need three times the ground force to cover this whole mountain in one hour."

Wild Bill held the phone away from his ear, cogitating. Then he spoke quickly into it. "Return to baseline."

The Major handed the instrument back to an aide, thought for another moment, and said, "Get everybody off the northern face. Call the dark side of the moon and tell them we're going to dust."

Lacombe emerged from the communications trailer and was holding a sports jacket on a cellophane-covered wire hanger. He walked across the pad toward a waiting transport helicopter, Laughlin trailing him. The Frenchman stopped to watch Wild Bill give the order to the E-Z-Four-loaded helicopters. They revved up to a screaming level, then one at a time the three choppers lifted off vertically and in follow-the-leader style headed up and off into the night, their red and green lights blinking.

The Frenchman gazed hard at Wild Bill, more in

sorrow than in anger. Then he followed Laughlin and five button-down civilian operators onto the Huey. The door was immediately slid shut and in a second the big cargo helicopter rose vertically and headed off into the night.

On the mountain, Roy, Jillian, and Larry were on the far side of exhaustion. They had worked their way nearly around to the back side of the mountain. From what Neary remembered of the model he had made, the box canyon couldn't be too far away. And he'd been right about the helicopters. They weren't dusting this section. So far.

A clearing lay ahead.

"Let's make a run for it," he said to Jillian and Larry.

Jillian simply nodded, saving her breath, but Larry, who was really shot, gasped, "Go ahead. I'll catch up."

"All right," Roy said. "We'll wait for you on the other side."

He took off running, crouched low to the ground, Jillian right behind him. In less than a minute, they had made it across the open space and thrown themselves down on the pine needles, panting and gasping. They were very thirsty, dripping with perspiration, and their hands and faces stung from numberless bramble and branch slaps. Somewhere along the line, perhaps in the helicopter door, Neary had damaged his left arm and shoulder. When he stopped to think about it, he was in considerable pain, and he was starting to lose the use of the arm.

They lay on their stomachs, looking for Larry.

"There!" Jillian whispered, pointing off to the left. They watched Butler emerge from the tree cover a good hundred yards downwind of them.

"Larry!" Roy called. "Over here!"

A perfectly terrible explosion of noise and light overwhelmed his call as an assault chopper trimmed the treetops, its powerful belly-light sweeping across the clearing.

Roy and Jillian stood up now, waving Larry toward them. The noise grew louder, but Neary shouted anyway, "You're in the clear . . . he'll spot you."

The helicopter swooped over, making a sharp bank above them. It must have seen the man in the clearing.

Larry had heard both the chopper and Neary, because he shouted up to them, using valuable lung power, "So what's he gonna do? Land on me?"

The helicopter came down over them and then headed for the clearing below. Small birds started dropping out of treetops off to the side. Neary and Jillian realized that they had to get upwind of the stuff. And fast. They were only fifty yards from the notch. Too exhausted to do anything more, they began crawling.

Behind them, the helicopter hovered, screaming, right over Larry. He seemed totally unconcerned in the middle of the noise, the little cyclone of needles, brush, and leaves, and the invisible E-Z Four. He stuck up his thumb, like a hitchhiker, and yelled, "Look, they're only cropdusting."

By the time Roy and Jillian had painfully crawled their way to the summit of the notch and looked back down. Larry Butler, still walking, was starting to twitch spasmodically. First his head, then his arms. He started to stagger.

Jillian started to get up. She was going to run down to him. Neary grabbed her. "No, no!" he shouted in her ear. "Don't look down." Jillian sank back.

They watched Larry fall, try to get up, twitch horribly on the open ground and then lie still.

They stood there, gazing out into the clearing. The tall grass was down in one place where Larry's body lay. "We shouldn't just leave him out there," Jillian said at last.

"If he's sleeping, he can do it there as well as here."

"And if he's dying?" Jillian asked.

"If he's dying"—Neary took another breath, then expelled it with a puffing sound—"then so are we."

Jillian's arm gave him a squeeze.

They moved off through the tall pines, heading toward the ridge. The way Neary remembered it, sculptured in mud and newspaper and chicken wire, the ridge provided a kind of gallery that ran around the canyon, a place shrouded by trees.

Even before they reached the ridge, a strong light seemed to be coming from just below it, a steady glow reflecting back in the dark night from tiny droplets of water vapor in the high, clear air. As they neared the edge, they dropped to their bellies and snaked forward for a cautious peek.

It was an uphill crawl along a thirty-foot stretch of slope. Neary could hear the helicopter coming back around the mountain. He reached for a scrawny bush to get a handhold, missed.

He slid back down the slope. "Roy!" Jillian called from her position at the top of the ridge. "Come on, Roy! You can make it!"

He was sweating. His legs ached. His fingers couldn't seem to grip. "Please, Roy! The helicopter's coming."

Neary squinted up at her. Jillian was reaching down the slope for his hand. He began to crawl. The agony of it took his breath away. Inches at a move through loose-packed, sandy dirt. Inches.

"Roy, just a few feet more and we can slide down the other side."

The chopper's *rat-a-tat* was louder. Sweat poured down Neary's forehead and into his eyes. He was only a yard from Jillian's outstretched hand. Half a yard.

The beat of the rotors filled the air overhead. At any moment the hissing sound of gas would come. Neary's whole body buckled convulsively. He threw himself forward. Jillian caught his hand.

She helped pull him up over the rim of the slope. They tumbled head over heels down a reverse incline and came to rest at the very rim of the canyon below.

The helicopter yammered past. Neary stared up at it through sweat-smeared eyes. No spray. They were too close to the canyon. They were safe.

He let out a great, shuddering sigh and took in a big lungful of fresh air. Then he and Jillian moved forward to stare over the brink of the canyon. Together they reached the edge of the outcropped plateau and peered over. Below was a sight they could not absorb.

"Christ!" Neary breathed.

"Oh, God!" Jillian cried. "Oh, my God!"

25

Nature had ended and Man had taken over.

It looked like an airport, a sort of cosmic port of call, manufactured by humans. There were landing lights stretching out to the horizon, perhaps five miles away, Neary estimated. Right in the center of the whole incredible base, the runway lights led up to a huge lighted double cross that was ringed by small strobe lights. It looked to Neary like a place where something was supposed to set down.

The entire area, which had been dynamited and bulldozed flat, was ringed by big stadium lights perched on metal standards. Under the brilliant lights, Roy and Jillian could see that the whole base was circumscribed by a six-foot-high steel retaining wall. Inside there were three levels and on each level there were many self-contained modular cubicles, all with two doors, some with big picture windows and some without windows. The cubicles were of different sizes and heights, perched on metal scaffolds and reached by ladders.

Upfield and in the center of the huge arena was a color-sound scoreboard that must have been forty feet long and six feet high, standing on a sixteen-foot scaffold and connected by many cables and conduits to a big ARP synthesizer on the ground downfield.

Without turning, Neary said, "Do you see that?"

"Oh, yes!" Jillian whispered.

"Good," Roy said, relieved to have received confirmation that he was not hallucinating or at least that he was not hallucinating alone.

They were two hundred, perhaps three hundred feet above the great open-ended stadium that had been blasted and carved out of the box canyon, and as their eyes and minds adjusted to the fantastic scene below, Roy and Jillian, without saying anything more, decided to scramble down lower and closer. They moved cautiously down the granite edges to a perch some fifty feet below where the brush provided excellent cover.

Now they could make out men, technicians apparently, working in and around the cubicles. They were dressed in jumpsuits—the white ones had *McDonnell-Douglas* written on the backs, the blue, *Rockwell,* and the red, *Lockheed.* The cubicles seemed to be set up as small laboratories. Roy and Jill could not make out what all the equipment was for, but they did recognize some laser apparatus, biochemical instruments, devices for thermal and electromagnetic measurements, looking like bazookas on their tripods, a couple of spectrographic analyzers, and a lot of complicated-looking instruments intended to monitor and measure God only knew what.

Inside three of the cubicles sat black-suited men, all wearing dark glasses, guarded by military personnel, the only military that Neary could spot. Around the base were great radar dishes, constantly panning around and occasionally stopping for a moment and then moving on again. There were television monitors everywhere and at least a hundred film cameras, fifty still cameras and twenty-five videotape TV cameras set in banks on swivels. There were perhaps thirty operators and loaders for all cameras; the rest evidently were operated by remote control and connected to the tracking radar.

Despite its size, the area was both cluttered and a mess. There were Coca-Cola and snack food machines scattered about indiscriminately, portable outhouses around the perimeter, and a small catering area that reminded Roy of an army soup kitchen under a canvas overhang. There were a lot of unopened crates that had *McDonnell-Douglas*, *Rockwell*, and *Lockheed* markings on the sides, and there was debris— paper cups, napkins, plates, empty soda cans everywhere. In fact, some guys in jumpsuits were sweeping up the stuff just as an apparent tour of executives in sunglasses, led by a white-haired man in a jumpsuit, strolled by.

A bunch of technicians were clustered around the synthesizer, and one character, at the urging of the others, sat down at the large console and began pick-

ing out "Moon River" with one finger. The squeals
and wows echoed across the canyon and vague forms
of light and color shifted and faded across the giant
scoreboard. The "musician" was shouted down by
other technicians across the gridiron.

"I know what this is!" Neary said, more to himself
than to Jillian. "I know what this is! This is unbelievable!"

A gentle chime sounded below them.

"Gentlemen, ladies—"

A voice came over the loudspeaker system. He
must have been in one of the cubicles, perhaps the
communications cubicle, the one with all the computers. No, now they saw him.

A fellow in a white jumpsuit, holding a small microphone, the cord trailing out behind him, was walking out to the center of the arena. "Gentlemen, ladies.
Take your positions, please. This is not a drill. I repeat: This is not a drill. Could we have the lights in
the arena down sixty percent? Sixty percent, please."

Gradually the stadium lights started dimming, and
the landing lights were dialed up. For five miles down
the strip—all the way to the horizon—Roy and Jillian
watched the lights come up. Suddenly they noticed
that inside the modules the computer and instrument
lights were going from white to red. Red working
lights were now glowing from almost all the cubicles.

"Good, good, good," the man who was acting like
a master of ceremonies enthused. "I don't think we

could ask for a more beautiful evening. Do you? Well, if everyone is ready—"

Neary understood that these several hundred scientists and technicians had been holding a vigil every night for some time, and every night had been a false alarm. Nothing had happened. No one had come. Now he noticed that all the radar dishes had stopped sweeping and were focused in one direction, directly at them.

"They're staring at us," Jillian gasped, scrunching down even flatter on the rock.

"Not at us. At the sky. Look."

Roy and Jill turned their faces to the stars.

Something was beginning.

At first, Neary and Jillian had no idea what it was. Their eyes slowly adjusted from the glare of the stadium lights to the almost total darkness above them. The first thing they picked out was the Milky Way, then in the northern sky they saw the constellation of Orion. They stared hard at the cluster of stars they had seen so often before.

They were moving. The stars were moving.

The stars that made up the constellation shifted slowly at first, then more rapidly, some edging away, leaving the constellation.

Neary turned to search the sky. He found another Orion at the opposite horizon.

"There's the real one," he said, pointing it out to Jillian.

When they looked back at the changing Orion, it had already become something different, its "stars," which clearly were not stars, shifting constantly. A number of them had moved until they had formed an almost evenly spaced curved line. Then from the end "star," as if attracted by it, three more moved in with majestic speed to form an oblong shape.

The Big Dipper.

Neary started laughing. He was no longer afraid at all. He was just very happy.

Below them, the hundreds of scientists and technicians were reacting like ordinary mortals at a show of fireworks, *oohhing* and *aahhing* and finally bursting into applause when the Dipper was fully formed.

"We're the only ones who know. The only ones," Roy said. "Did you see that?" he asked her, checking.

"Yes," Jillian reassured him and herself.

"Good."

All of a sudden what appeared to be three shooting stars came out of the western sky. They shot right overhead and abruptly stopped, as if putting on brakes, in midspace, exploding in a moment every known law of physics. The stars executed—on a dime —a complete 180-degree turn and then each point of light broke off into four different points and shot back off into the night sky.

Inside the stadium the audience went wild.

Roy and Jill looked at each other.

"Did you see *that?*"

"Yes."

"Good."

The show was not over. It was, in fact, just beginning.

A cloud, what appeared to be a simple, lonely cloud, floated over the base, escorted by two very bright blue points of light within it. The two blue lights began to swirl faster and faster around the cloud, which started losing its form and reshaped itself into a nebula that resembled a spiral nebula.

One of the lights penetrated the nebula and turned on even more brightly so that the whole cloud was lit up from within. No longer blue, but a deep amber. And then the other light took up a position in the outer arm of the spiral and began blinking on and off.

It was an extraordinary sight, a vision that seemed to flash and swirl with meaning, if only they could apprehend it. It was a demonstration, there was no doubt of that. But a cosmic demonstration of what? Of the place in the cosmic galaxy where we live? Yes! Perhaps that was it. A scale model of our planet's location. Incredible!

Roy and Jillian did not speak. They were trying to catch their breaths, trying to assimilate these sights and perceptions. They were crouched on a small promontory. Behind them was nothing, just the night sky and distance. Suddenly, in that sky, were clouds moving on both sides behind them. And from the clouds a light—like heat lightning except when the light flashed stroboscopically it did not go off. The flash froze midsky.

Then the light got brighter still in one part of the cloud, and bursting out of the cloud came an intensely bright pencil point of orange light, followed by two more brilliant pencil points of orange light. In a moment, as the lights approached an unbelievable speed in a sort of wing formation, Neary and Jillian just had time to cover their faces as the vehicles made a slow, screaming pass right over their heads.

They were the same ones—the monster klieg lights, the flashing, beautifully colored sunset, the enormous jack-o'-lantern with its leering, phantom face—that had appeared so spectacularly to them on the Indiana summit so many nights ago.

As these enormous furnace lights—vehicles without wings or physics, brilliant, flashing, colored lights that blew away one's security, the belief in your own existence and that of the "real" world—passed over them, a huge displacement of air and heat blew dust everywhere. Their hair went in all directions, the static electricity made all the hair on Neary's arms and chest stand up on end.

Again they felt buffeted and seared by the heat. Again the very breath was sucked out of their lungs. They had just enough time to inhale as each of the three vehicles, wailing mournfully like a million banshees, swept over. This time the sounds they made were frightening. A thousand voices wailing, sending chills up their backs right in the middle of the intense heat. Neary realized that the sounds were the noises of foreign machinery, but this realization did not make him feel any more secure.

By the time Roy and Jill had cleared the dust and the tears from their eyes, the monstrous, flashing, brilliantly colored vehicles were swooping low over the stadium area, sending the scoreboard off into a riot of colors and the scientists and technicians scuttling for cover. The cameras followed the objects on their swivels and the radar dishes panned all the way round.

The brilliant objects passed over the double-cross landing area that was flashing landing coordinates to them, swooped several hundred yards further down the concrete strip where there was nobody around, abruptly stopped as if putting on brakes and then just . . . hovered.

They hovered in a sort of triangle formation, their brilliant, almost-impossible-to-look-at colors holding steady. The objects seemed to settle close to the tarmac, perhaps as close as five feet above it, then they would pop back up to about twenty-five feet. They seemed to be almost flirting with the ground, playing, tasting it, licking up some dirt and debris, but then popping up as if actually frightened.

Neary was bug-eyed. He wanted to climb down closer to it all but realized that Jillian was too freaked out to move.

Meanwhile, something that Roy realized had been planned and rehearsed and rehearsed a hundred, a thousand times for just this historical moment, began to unfold. The synthesizer was surrounded and boarded by a group of technicians wearing headsets and pencil microphones that they plugged into the console. Trailing their twenty-foot cords, they gathered around with their clipboards and penlights in hand.

One man, obviously the team leader, said into the almost-reverent hush, "All right, gentlemen. Shall we begin?"

In the communications booth, a technician spoke into his pencil mike. "TC stereo. Time and resistance . . . Auto ready. Tone interpolation on interlock."

Another technician said, "ARP interlock now! Speed set at seven and a half. All positive functions standing by. Sunset!"

"Go."

Lacombe and David Laughlin, clad in white jumpsuits, also stood by the console of the synthesizer. Sitting now before the double keyboard was a young man who resembled William Shakespeare. He was obviously very nervous, perspiring heavily, wiping his face and hands on a handkerchief, clearly aware of the tremendous responsibility that lay upon him.

The master of ceremonies said softly to him, "Okay. Start with the tone."

Shakespeare played the first note.

The booth technician spoke into his pencil microphone. "Tang . . . go!"

An amber light appeared on the giant scoreboard,

fading and disappearing as the note floated away across the canyon.

"Up a full tone," the M.C. ordered, and Shakespeare sounded the second note.

The scoreboard lit up a deep pink.

"Down a major third."

A new note and a new color. Violet, this time.

"Now drop an octave."

The fourth note echoed and a beautiful, deep blue played across the scoreboard.

"Cool blue . . . Go," the booth technician ordered.

"Up a perfect fifth," the M.C. said.

The last note sounded and faded away. The scoreboard flashed a brilliant red and faded.

"Nothing. Nothing at all," the team leader said.

The M.C. said to Shakespeare, "Give me a tone."

A note sounded, a color flashed, and the five-note-five-color sequence was repeated, according to the M.C.'s instructions.

In the booth, the technician ordered, "*Re* to the second. *Me* to the third. *Do* the first. *Do* one-half one. *Sol* to the fifth."

The notes and the colors faded away across the arena, and there was still no response from the three objects. They just hovered downfield, flashing and blinking inscrutably.

Lacombe stepped up to the console and said, "*Encore une fois.* Again. One more time."

The five-note sequence sounded and echoed

through the night and the five colors played and danced across the scoreboard.

"Speak to me, speak to me," the team leader pleaded.

"*Plus vite,*" Lacombe commanded. "*Plus vite.*"

Shakespeare did as he was ordered. This time the notes and the colors cascaded around the arena.

High above on their ledge, Jillian Guiler hummed the five-note sequence through twice. "I know that," she told Neary. Oh, my God, she thought. It's Barry's song. Jill was almost in shock, tears in her eyes, but Roy didn't notice.

Below, Lacombe was saying, "Faster, Jean Claude. Faster. *Plus vite.* Faster." He started walking down the landing strip toward the hovering vehicles. "*Plus vite. Plus vite.*"

The sweat was really pouring off Shakespeare now, dripping onto the keys of the synthesizer. He was playing the notes very fast and loud now, and the scoreboard was zooming from amber to pink to purple to blue to red.

Lacombe walked up the strip to within one hundred and fifty yards of the hovering, nonresponding vehicles. The booth technician dialed the synthesizer all the way up and the notes reverberated hugely off the walls of the canyon.

The Frenchman had become very impatient. "*Qu'est-ce qui se passe?*" he asked the objects. "*Allez, allez, allez. Allons-y.* Let's go." Lacombe was shouting over the moog, making the five-note hand movements.

Lacombe waved his hands at the hovering vehicles and called to the musician, *"Plus vite, plus vite,"* then headed back toward the console.

Shakespeare was playing his brains out and the scoreboard was flashing through the colors of the spectrum from ultraviolet to infrared and everything in between.

All of a sudden the vehicles responded. Not in sounds but in colors. They began to repeat the colors on the scoreboard. Each object was repeating separately the colors flashing across the board. Shakespeare stopped playing. As the notes faded away across the canyon, there was utter silence. For a long moment, all they could hear was the wind blowing down the canyon.

Then Lacombe pointed to Shakespeare and said, "Come on. Keep going, keep going."

The team leader exhorted his man on. "Kick that mule, boy!"

The musician/engineer began playing very, very quickly and the scoreboard and the three vehicles picked up the action, changing colors in the same variation in total synchrony. The men around him were all sweating profusely, too, concentrating fiercely as the objects flashed their colors. They were filled with joy. In fact, they were beyond joy. In a state that no humans had previously experienced or described. For this was the first contact, the first contact in recorded history.

And suddenly the three objects stopped responding.

They just flew off. In three different directions. One shot straight up and disappeared, lights off, apparently, into a large cloud. The other two swooped over the edge of the canyon and out of sight.

The music stopped. The scoreboard went to black. Silence. The wind.

And then the arena went crazy. Everyone began applauding and screaming. These restrained, calm scientists and technicians were jumping up and down, hugging each other, shaking hands, pounding each other on the backs. The stadium lights came back on full, and the men in their jumpsuits and civilian clothes started coming out of their cubicles. Everything, it seemed, was over.

The booth technicians came down and sought out Lacombe and the team leader.

"Beautiful," he said. "Beautiful."

Lacombe spoke to David Laughlin in English. "I am very happy tonight."

The team leader shook all their hands, including Shakesepare's. "Congratulations. Not Merle Haggard, but it was great!"

Above this scene of jubilation, on their rocky ledge, Roy was completely elated and Jillian in tears. "I know that sound," she kept on saying. "I just know it. I've heard it, I know that sound."

Below, in one of the radar communications cubicles, the instruments started showing targets. The deep dish radar scoops had stopped sweeping again, focusing on the mountain above Neary and Jillian. Something was happening in the sky beyond Devil's Tower.

On the floor of the stadium, one of the technicians approached the Frenchman, saying, "Mr. Lacombe," and pointed up.

Lacombe and Laughlin walked away looking up at the sky.

"What is it?" David Laughlin asked. "What's happening?"

"*Je ne sais pas.*"

Roy and Jill turned, looking back and up toward where the men below were now all looking and pointing. Then they saw it, too.

A number of large cumulus clouds had formed in the sky over the mountain. Within the clouds was an extraordinary display of flashing pyrotechnics—an electrical storm different from anything that they had seen before and frightening in its scale and turbulence.

Simultaneously, and without words, Neary and Jillian felt that they must get away from the sky, so together they started the perilous scramble down. Jillian was terrified. The flashing clouds suddenly reminded her of the awful day that Barry was taken.

The clouds had come down very close to the top of the mountain. There seemed to be more of them now. Suddenly zooming out of the clouds, one of the brilliantly lighted objects swept down across the arena, stopping just where it had hovered before. It hovered

again and then suddenly flashed all its lights. Red.
Three times.

It was, evidently, a signal of some kind.

The largest part of the cloud formation flashed red
three times. Then it flashed white and blue three
times.

There was a brief pause during which all the technicians looked at each other uneasily. What the hell
next?

Then the invasion began.

Out of the clouds burst a formation of fifty pinpoints of light that swiftly materialized into flaming
convex planar shapes and dazzling colors. And tricks.
These ultra-performance vehicles were performing
low-level stunts for their audience.

Three of them stopped in midair and fell toward
the ground. Just when it seemed that there must be a
tremendous impact, they came to a complete stop
and hovered, causing a huge displacement of air that
thundered and roared and rumbled across the canyon.

The objects were making no sounds by themselves
now, but their gravity-defying maneuvers were creat-
ing thunder that rattled the cubicles, the instruments
within, short-circuiting several of the computers, and
everyone's brains. The lights! The heat! So hot that
some of the paper debris caught fire as the vehicles
carried out their low, swooshing passes over the field.

They played games. Two formations headed break-
neck straight ahead toward each other. Just as a
massive head-on collision seemed inevitable, the ob-

jects somehow filtered through each other, sweeping up, barrel-rolling and swooping back down again.

Gradually, a new thing—resembling the bottom of an electric griddle, bright red and blinking—moved out over the base at an agonizingly slow five miles per hour. It was traveling very low and sucking up—apparently magnetically—everything loose that was metal: clipboards, pens, spectacles, and headsets right off the technicians' heads, cigarette lighters out of their pockets, soda pop cans. One fellow grabbed his mouth as a loose filling flew out of his dental work and stuck to the bottom of the griddle fryer.

Suddenly, the vehicle flashed a blue color, and everything it had sucked up was let go and fell in a pile onto the ground.

Iacombe walked casually over after it had released its booty and stuck his hand up. The Frenchman walked directly under the strange thing, reached up and actually touched its bottom. It was not hot, but it must have been ticklish, for as soon as Lacombe touched it, it jumped up, scattering the technicians who had followed Lacombe with their cameras and heat-sensory devices and other instruments, and flew off toward the heavens so suddenly that it left behind an enormous thunderclap, which smashed several cubicle windows and scared the hell out of everyone.

Neary was more thrilled than scared. "I've got to get closer," he told her.

"I know you do," she said. "This is close enough for me."

"I've got to get down there. Won't you come just a little bit further?"

"No, Roy. I'll wait here."

"I gotta get down there," he said almost apologetically.

"I know," Jillian said. "I really know. I really know what you want to do."

They looked at each other closely, sadly. And for the first time since they had known each other they kissed.

Then they parted.

Jillian climbed thirty feet back up the cliff to a small wooded area where she felt she might be more protected and would not be seen by the figures below.

Neary started the long, dangerous scramble down.

26

As Roy clambered down the edge of the mountain, he noticed that the display was over. As though some signal had been given, all the objects receded into the night.

Now in the background, coming out of the low clouds, a hundred points of light flared up around the entire twenty-mile perimeter of the box canyon. Although these light points were hovering at least ten miles away, Neary could tell they were large nuts and bolts vehicles, just hanging there, seeming to guard the perimeter of the base. Now they rose up higher in the sky and dimmed their lights. Roy could barely make out the black shapes behind the glow.

Things got stranger still.

Down in the stadium, everyone was exhausted now, picking themselves up stunned silly. They had all been going through total culture shock, and each man was trying to deal with it in his own way.

There was no conversation. The wind had dropped off completely now, and the silence was total.

Neary had kept coming all this time and was now on the floor of the mountain, edging his way toward the perimeter of the base when something made him stop and look up.

From behind the mountain and from inside a cloud, something began coming out of the cloud that was completely black. It was not only black but it was huge. So huge that Roy could not comprehend its size. As the huge black shape came over the top of the mountain, blotting out the moon and casting a shadow that crawled over everybody in the canyon, Neary thought he was going to pass out.

Inside the base, the master of ceremonies murmured, "Oh, my God!"

"Holy shit!" Laughlin exclaimed, not hearing himself.

Lacombe stared, transfixed. *"Mon Dieu!"* he said, realizing that if they could measure this shape, this thing, that it would be over a mile wide and the length of it, covering the entire sky, was still unknown because the end of it was not in sight.

Suddenly it turned on. A surgical sliver of light circumscribed the underside of the thing, and then something opened—some round circle of light exploded.

It was the size of a city, Neary thought. The top of it looked like an oil refinery, with huge tanks and pipes and working lights everywhere. The phantom mass, sliding across the canyon, seemed somehow old and dirty. It looked junky, like an old city or an immense old ship that had been sailing the skies for thousands of years. Neither Roy nor any of the scientists or technicians—nor anyone else on earth, for that matter—had ever seen or even imagined anything like it.

As it came over the base, a huge explosion of light arced out behind it and separated into what looked like a thousand brilliant fireflies, except that each "firefly" was a small (by comparison) vehicle acting like a tugboat. Each "tugboat" flashed different colors and the thousand of them together formed a scaffold of many-colored lights onto which the phantom mass —two miles long and a mile wide—seemed to settle. The mass made a slight list as the scaffold—crossbeams blinking colors—escorted it to a landing area of its own far downfield.

Neary had vaulted over the six-foot retaining wall and was now wedged in among the technicians and scientists, all of whom were simply stunned by what they were seeing.

The scaffolding guided the mass down, shattering about a mile of the landing coordinate lights. It was so big that when it settled, the leading edge of the mass formed a roof over the top of the entire camp.

The mass had created its own negative gravity field, and within moments everyone and everything became 40 percent weightless. This cheered everyone. They started bouncing and cavorting buoyantly in the air, some of the more athletic doing cartwheels and somersaults, hanging in the air like Dr. J., their colleagues in jumpsuits sliding and bouncing beneath them with their cameras, snapping pictures of the whole incredible thing.

Some of the pinpoints of light-energy began to explore the area for themselves. The cuboids flickered in and out among the cavorting humans like fireflies traveling faster than the speed of light, making right-angle turns and generally violating any and all of Newton's laws of physics.

Neary watched one of them settle on the upturned palm of his hand, nesting into the skin like a snow-flake, a luminous one. He smiled down at the point of brightness, then in amazement watched it slip effortlessly through his skin and travel along a vein for a moment.

"I'll be damned," Neary breathed, watching the cuboid zigzag through his arteries, pick up a neural network, and fork its way back like a drunken flash of lightning along a nerve pathway that led out the middle finger of Neary's left hand.

A squadron of pinpoints began swarming over a Coke machine, darting in, out, and through it. One of the technicians inserted a coin, got out a can of Coke, and popped the fliptop open.

Cuboids dived headlong into the can. They emerged an instant later in wriggles and lopside spirals, curling motions, cross-hatching, fizzing explosions, and quickly executed figure eights, stars, and comets.

"This stuff really turns them on," one human laughed.

Two cuboids, high on Coke, disappeared down the inside of his shirt and began looping wild zigzags around his groin and midriff. "Fellas!" the human begged helplessly. "Hey, fellas, we're not even introduced."

"How'dy'know they're fellas?" a companion asked.

A platoon of cuboids, flashing a red streak, followed by yellow, pried open the Coke machine door and tumbled cans out onto the tarmac. Trooping in like waves of the sea, battalions of the energy-points swooped up the beverage and exploded in brilliant clouds.

They formed Mickey Mouse. Then Popeye. Then blacked out and reappeared a millimicrosecond later on the far side of the tarmac, bouncing one technician up and down as if on a blanket.

Neary found himself laughing with glee. Was this real, any of it? he wondered. Did it matter? It was like a school of kids let loose at recess time, rioting up and down the playground, trying one outrageous stunt after another.

One technician, stuffier than the rest, found a group of cuboids tugging at the pipe in his mouth. He resisted. They persisted. Yanking the pipe away from him, they swooped skyward, trailing sparks of tobacco.

The mother ship grunted softly.

In an instant the cuboids swarmed upward and disappeared. Silence.

The technicians snapped out of their gleeful trance

and began shuffling their minds back to the task at hand. Someone had the presence of mind to lock the Coke machine. But the experience had been too` intense. They stood about in dazed groups, trying hard to remember why they were there.

Lacombe and the team leader were the first to recover partially. They decided to move the synthesizer, which was mounted on casters, closer to the mass. After they had rolled it about seventy-five feet downfield, the members of the team, still feeling otherworldly and unglued, plugged themselves in again.

The master of ceremonies spoke as dispassionately as he could into his pencil microphone. "All departments at operational during this phase signify by beeping twice."

Two tones rang across the canyon, startling the utter silence.

The booth technician asked, "Is audio analyzer ready? On a standby?"

The master of ceremonies, regaining some equilibrium now that he was doing something, said, "If everything is ready here on the dark side of the moon, play the five tones."

Shakespeare played the five notes very slowly.

There was no response from the phantom mass.

"*Encore,*" Lacombe ordered.

The five notes sounded through the night.

The great ship made a sound. It sounded like a pig grunting.

"Must have been something she et," the team leader said nervously.

The musician/engineer started playing the five notes again.

No response at all this time.

"Again," the team leader said.

Shakespeare started playing.

Suddenly the last two notes were completed by the great mother ship. The noise was incredible. It blew the men back on their heels and shattered all the windows in all the cubicles. The booth technicians ducked the flying glass, and some were cut, but too involved even to notice.

"Okay," the team leader said, after a moment. "Play it again."

The synthesizer sounded and the ship responded. This time lights—matching the scoreboard's—flashed brilliantly across its surface.

Jillian Guiler knew she could not take any more of this alone. Frightened as she was, she felt it better to try to come down and find Neary. Jillian picked up her little satchel and her Instamatic camera and started climbing down, following the path that Roy had taken.

The master of ceremonies said to Shakespeare and the booth technician, "Give her six quavers, then pause."

The musician played the notes.

The ship echoed these notes and then played a

group of new notes that none of them had ever heard before.

The booth technician said, "She gave us four quavers. A group of five quavers. A group of four semiquavers."

Shakespeare imitated the ship's notes.

The ship added five new notes and five different colors.

Inside the computer cubicles, the technicians were in a state of Nirvana. The ship was teaching them their musical and chromal vocabulary.

As the exchanges increased in complexity and speed, the computers took over from Shakespeare. He took his hands away from the keys and the ARP was played by the computers, like a player piano.

"Take everything from the lady," the M.C. instructed the booth technician. "Follow her pattern note for note."

The mother ship exploded with sound and color and the ARP, in interlock with the computer and the color scoreboard, was playing right back. For several ecstatic minutes the great ship, the ARP, and the scoreboard were actually jamming, like some sort of cosmic rock and light show.

It was very strange music—at one moment melodic and the next atonal, sometimes jazzy, then a little country western, and the next moment something so grotesque and unmusical to their ears that they had to turn away.

Neary was smiling. He did not notice that Jillian was

now working her way through the crowd. Some of the technicians were clapping; some holding their heads. Lacombe had a dazed, glazed expression.

Suddenly, the ship stopped. It gave a few grunts, and then went silent. All its lights went out.

The base was deadly still and dark for a few moments.

And then the ship started opening.

The whole bottom end of it, beginning with a circumscribed sliver of surgical light, opened into a furnace of light.

Everyone turned away. They put on their dark glasses and turned back. But even through their sunglasses it was hard to look directly into that burning light.

The thing opened more.

That was too much. Everyone moved back fast. They moved away from the unnerving light, which was about one hundred and fifty yards wide.

The opening kept expanding.

First Lacombe, then Neary, and then the others stepped forward again. The white light gave off an intense heat, and then stopped.

Inside the bright heat they could see some movement.

The light was so bright that it flared out in all directions. Now there seemed to be eight different figures materializing out of the light. The white light devoured their forms into pipe cleaner shapes.

Then they were out of the ship and out of the light.

Lacombe walked toward them.

He—and the others—now saw that they were . . . men.

"I am Claude Lacombe," the Frenchman said to the group.

The men appeared utterly dazed. They were dressed in naval flak jackets of the forties. They were all very young and several of them were holding leather helmets and flight goggles in their hands.

They continued to walk forward numbly, in complete shock.

The first man stopped, half saluted, and said, "Frank Taylor. Lieutenant J.G. United States Navy Reserve, 064199."

The M.C. stepped forward and shook his hand. "Lieutenant, welcome home. This way to debriefing."

Two men led the lieutenant away.

Neary was having difficulty taking all this in. He noticed for the first time a large lightboard with perhaps a hundred black-and-white photographs fixed to it.

"Harry Ward Craig. Captain, United States Navy, 043431."

"Captain, would you come right this way?"

"Welcome back, Navy," the team leader said. "Welcome back."

"Craig, Harry Ward," a man in a civilian suit said. "Captain, United States Navy, 043431," another said, consulting a clipboard. "Disappeared off Chicken Shoals. Flight Number 19."

The first civilian went over to the lightboard and put a piece of tape over Craig's picture.

"Matthew McMichael. Lieutenant, United States Naval Reserve, 0909411."

"Lieutenant. Good to have you back."

Now more and more figures were emerging out of the intense light.

One of the civilians, staggered by it all, said to the team leader, "They haven't even aged! Einstein *was* right."

"Einstein was probably one of them."

There were now more than two hundred dazed returnees coming out of the great carrier. Immediately corralled by technicians, medical personnel, and some civilian officials, they were taken to the windowless cubicles. On top of each cubicle, Neary noticed, was a sling and hook. He guessed that the people, cubicles and all, would be airlifted away by the big army helicopters when all this was over.

As Roy turned back, he saw Jillian Guiler rushing forward. A tiny figure about three feet tall was running out of the light. It was Barry.

Jillian was laughing and crying as she charged forward. She embraced the boy, crying, "Yes! Yes!"

Barry hugged back. Neary, standing away from them, was shaking from excitement.

Jillian carried the little boy off to the side. They sat together on a little table, and Barry said, "I went up in the air and I saw our house."

"I saw you going up in the air," Jillian told him. "Did you see me running after you?"

"Yeah."

Roy Neary walked over to Lacombe, who had not noticed him until now. The Frenchman was delighted that Neary had made it this far.

"Monsieur Neary," he said, "what do you want?"

"I just want to know it's really happening."

Lacombe thought that just the right answer, because the Frenchman was convinced that Neary was a critical factor in this historic event. He left Neary standing there, looking at the great ship, and went over to where David Laughlin and several of the Mayflower Project officials were gathered.

"We have to speak about Mr. Neary's case," Lacombe began in French.

As Laughlin translated, they all noticed that the ship's huge opening was starting to close.

Barry saw it too. "Are they going away?" he asked his mother.

"Yes, they're going away, Barry. Are you going to stay with me?" Jillian asked him.

"Yes."

"Forever and ever till you grow up."

The little boy just laughed delightedly.

Lacombe, Laughlin, and the Mayflower officials were having a heated argument, all talking simultaneously.

Laughlin put up his hand for quiet, and said, "He

says these are ordinary people under extraordinary circumstances. They are *not* special cases."

Lacombe spoke rapidly again in French.

Translating, Laughlin said, "These people have given up their lives, their families to come all the way to this meeting. They have been implanted with the knowledge of this place. Their initiative and confidence brought them here. Now it is very important that Mr. Neary, as quickly as possible and voluntarily, be made a part of this project."

The ship's opening had closed completely.

Barry started to cry. "Good-bye," he called. "Goodbye." He waved, and Jillian started to cry, too.

Apparently, Lacombe had made his case successfully, because the Frenchman left the group and approached Roy again. He shook the bewildered American's hand, and said, "Monsieur Neary, I envy you."

At that moment, the great ship opened up again with an explosion of light and sound. BING-BONG it went. BING-BONG, as if calling for attention. All the metal in the base rattled at those brutal tones.

Something was coalescing again in the fiery interior of the star ship. Swirling bursts of energy were coming together, twining in helix forms until they seemed to . . . jell.

A figure stood there. Then another. Then a third.

They took a step forward. A single note of sound shot out of the carrier ship like the blare of a thousand trumpets. The three figures took another step forward.

They were immense, eight or nine feet tall. Terribly thin. Too thin for the inner mechanics of the human body, except they resembled humans because they moved on things like legs and waved things like arms.

Jillian picked up a protesting Barry and started moving swiftly away toward the rear of the base. She wasn't taking any chances again. She'd thought she could face anything now that she had Barry, but these creatures were too much.

They took another step forward and then stopped and touched each other. When they touched, they started to glow all over, light was shooting out from their figures. They stood there, touching, swaying, glowing, and then one of them seemed to reach out an incredible long armlike thing and pointed it at Roy.

Neary seemed confused and moved several steps away from the armlike thing. But it followed, seeming to hone in on him. It was definitely pointing at him.

Now Lacombe was also pointing at Roy, nodding at him encouragingly.

The M.C. said, "Mr. Neary, I am told we can count on your complete cooperation. What type of blood do you have?"

"I don't have the slightest idea," Neary said.

The M.C. led Roy over to one of the cubicles. They entered it.

"What is your date of birth?"

"December 4, 1945."

"Have you ever been inoculated against smallpox, diphtheria . . .? Is there any history of liver disease in your family?"

Jillian, carrying Barry in her arms and her small satchel over one shoulder, had left the base camp and was climbing back to the mountain when she heard a new sound below her and turned to look back down.

From within the huge space vehicle a great twittering sound emerged. The space within seemed to convulse, writhing with energy. Small forms began to emerge and make their way through the fiery opening.

They seemed about three feet high, humanoid in that they had arms and legs and a kind of bulbous head. But each figure was hard to distinguish because it was silhouetted against the fiery yellow-white furnace of the mother craft. Their arms and legs were incredibly flexible in a way no human could imitate.

They were infinitely extensible, too, as Lacombe soon discovered. One of the tiny visitors wrapped an arm around him and the arm kept growing longer until it completely encircled the Frenchman's waist.

At first, there was a certain tentativeness about the visitors. They seemed to be testing their shapes against those of the humans, but they also seemed to be testing the reception the humans would give them.

Touch was the key. They touched everywhere, everything. And since touch is something humans react to differently, some of the jumpsuited technicians recoiled and some responded in friendlier fashion.

Inside one of the larger cubicles, which had been designed to resemble a small chapel, a strange service was taking place. Twelve men, in red jumpsuits, holding helmets, with life-support packs on their backs, were kneeling in front of another man dressed in a white jumpsuit.

Beside him stood Lacombe, eyeing the volunteer astronauts. "Before the prayer," he said in slow, careful English, "let me say only this."

He paused and looked into each of their faces. "When you go to—" He stopped. "How shall I say it? When you go *on the other side*. That is a condition, a state of being we know nothing about."

He tried to smile in an encouraging manner. "You will lose touch with the entity that once was you." He continued in his slow, measuring tone. "There will be many claims on your attention, your loyalty, your intelligence, your faith."

Their eyes stared widely into his. Several of them swallowed nervously. "This one thing you must remember," Lacombe concluded. "You must never lose yourself so utterly that you do not remember from whence you came. You are us. You are our couriers, our delegates, our representatives. And one day, *you will return.*"

The astronauts' faces seemed to brighten at this. "Yes," Lacombe assured them, "only remember who you are. On the other side it will be. fascinating. Seductive. Exciting. But you will never forget that we who sent you are expecting your return." He glanced sideways at the priest in the white jumpsuit. "Father?"

"May the Lord be praised at all times," the priest intoned.

"May God grant us a happy journey," the astronauts responded.

"Lord, show us your ways."

"And lead us along your path."

"Oh, that our lives be bent."

"And keeping our precepts."

In another cubicle, Neary was now dressing in a red jumpsuit similar to the astronauts'.

"Mr. Neary," the M.C. was saying, "our staff has prepared a few basic documents that need your signature. This first just states that you have requested special status within the Mayflower Project of your own volition and have not been coerced into participating."

Outside, the touching was not only general now, but specific. The visitors were feeling human groins, human faces, human backsides. If the human didn't like it, they moved on to someone who did. And if the human responded by touching them back, the humanoid visitors seemed to swoon for an instant, blinking through a dozen colors and vibrating from dark to bright.

Once they realized they were among "friends," the humanoids turned loose in an orgy of touching, palpating, feeling, stroking.

On a ledge above this extraordinary happening, Jillian and Barry watched. Jillian dug into her satchel and took out her little camera. She started snapping away. Barry was giggling again, telling his mother about his little friends below.

Lacombe seemed to be a center of general humanoid affection, probably because he was responding tactilely, stroking when stroked, touching when touched. He was laughing. David Laughlin, beside him, was also similarly engaged.

Inside the chapel, the priest was still intoning, "God has given you his angels' charge over you. Grant these pilgrims, we pray, a happy journey." But the twelve astronauts' attention had wandered to the large window. They could see and hear snatches of the extraordinary goings-on outside. Not even their years of training had prepared them for all this. To a man, they were all very frightened.

Inside Neary's cubicle, the M.C. was still going on. "This last document is merely a formality. You see, we have a possible problem in the area of canon and common jurisprudence outside of the parameters of our astronomy. The case could be made that you are, in effect, technically speaking . . . dead. This paper just certifies that should such a judgment be rendered, that you will accept it. It's merely a formality."

Roy didn't know what the hell the guy was talking about or what papers he found himself signing.

He caught sight of the twelve astronauts filing out of the chapel, and then he and the master of ceremonies left their cubicle and joined the procession. The M.C. kept on briefing him feverishly, giving him a cassette player and a satchel full of tapes. A medical technician was listening to his heart through a stethoscope while they walked, and someone else was checking the electrodes in his suit and testing the portable transmitter that was hooked up through a battery pack to the computers in the medical cubicle.

Now the priest was chanting again. "By the guidance of a star, grant these pilgrims, we pray, a happy journey and peaceful days so that with Your divine angel as their guide they may reach their destination and finally come to the haven of everlasting salvation. God, who led Your servant Abraham out of Ur of the Chaldeans and kept him safe in all his wanderings, may it please You, we pray, also to watch over these servants of Yours."

The procession was now surrounded by dozens of little visitors, chittering and blinking. Obviously, they wanted the line to halt.

The priest stopped walking, but continued chanting in a louder monotone. Clearly, he was also very, very frightened. "Be to them, Lord, a help in their preparations, comfort on the way, shade in the heat, shelter in the rain and cold, a carriage in tiredness, a shield in adversity, a staff in insecurity, a haven in shipwreck, so that under Your guidance they may happily reach their destination and finally return safe to their homes."

Two of the humanoids entwined themselves around Roy and separated him from the others. Then they left him standing there alone, as if free to make up his mind. Neary turned, looking for Jillian and Barry, but he couldn't find them. Then he spotted Lacombe. They looked at each other a long moment, and the Frenchman nodded his head encouragingly and smiled.

Roy turned and took the first step forward. Then he started walking slowly, then faster toward the ship's negative gravity zone, and the fiery, lighted opening. The twelve astronauts began to follow him.

The little humanoids formed a blinking, twittering file on either side of the column of astronauts and accompanied them up the brilliantly lighted stairway toward the glowing interior of the great mother ship.

One little creature separated himself from the procession and flowed over to Lacombe. He reached out one armlike thing and made the first of the hand signs, corresponding to the first note. Lacombe, deeply moved, responded. Then the creature and the Frenchman went through the other four hand signs.

Lacombe looked down into its . . . face. It was changing—from something embryonic, unformed, into a face of something a thousand years old. Suddenly, Lacombe knew that all the wisdom, all the superintelligence, the experience that it had to take to build these vehicles, to travel these dozens of light years was there in the aging countenance and the . . . yes, the smile of this fantastic little creature. Lacombe smiled back, and then the little thing flowed away after the others into the phantom ship.

Neary was almost inside now. Incredibly, he was thinking and hearing a song in his head. It was from *Pinocchio.*

When you wish upon a star,
Makes no difference who you are.
Anything your heart desires will come . . . to . . . you.

He took another step up the ramp of fiery brilliance into the center of the starship. Around him the blaze was almost blinding, yet he seemed to be able to see . . . everything. And the music in his head grew louder.

If your heart is in your dream,
No request is too extreme,
When you wish upon a star as dreamers do.

Roy turned to make sure the twelve astronauts were still with him. Then he waved one last time to Lacombe and to Jillian and Barry. He hoped they could still see him.

Outside, on the cement strip, the figures of Neary, the astronauts, the little creatures, were dematerializing into fiery light and energy.

Like a bolt out of the blue,
Fate steps in and sees you through.
When you wish upon a star your dream . . .
    comes . . . true.

Neary walked forward again, leading the way deep into the fiery heart of the mystery.

He was in a corridor of such wild brilliance that his eyes ached. Slowly, he made his way forward, almost weightless now. He seemed to float as he put one foot ahead of the other.

Ahead of him a dark trapezoidal shape loomed larger with each step. It seemed an end to the fiery corridor, an entrance into . . . something darker.

Taking a single step into the new darkness, Neary looked around him. His eyes slowly adjusted, pupils widening to take in the fact that he stood at the outer perimeter of an immense circular area.

It was vast, at least a hundred yards across, a round room with a low ceiling that barely cleared Neary's head. He reached up to touch it. The feel was warm, metallic, but carrying a kind of surface charge that made his fingers tingle. He withdrew his hand and stood there, surveying the scene.

As he did so, he became aware that the light was growing brighter. Around the circumference of the room, six trapezoidal entrances stood, like the one through which he had stepped. Light grew in each opening.

Abruptly, a noise came from the center of the room. It was a strange sound, mechanical, Neary thought, something like the noise a telephone dial makes as it ratchets back to rest. Something too, he decided, like the ethereal beeps and drones of a long-distance call. Each sound intermingled with the others in a kind of medley that shifted with each second.

The sounds seemed to come from a circle of light imbedded in the center of the floor. Beams and colors flickered there in tempo with the sounds. A moment later, from the ceiling overhead, another centered circle sprang into life, pulsating with colors and emitting the same strange, almost conversational, tones.

The circles chattered. Light beams shot up from the floor, down from the ceiling. Laser-thin rays of intense light switched this way and that as the circles . . . talked . . . with each other. Yes, Neary decided, they were conversing in sounds and lights and colors.

Walking like stilts, beams marched back and forth around the circles, interrogating, answering, questioning, responding. The colors switched from orange and pink to blue and green. Finally three bright lasers of red, blue, and white shone fiercely down. An instant later the same rays shot up from the floor.

Silence. The light show died away.

A sharp metallic "klannng" from the left. Neary's head swiveled in time to see two immense metallic objects set in the wall between two openings rock up and click into place against the ceiling, bright lights pulsating around them. They seemed like gigantic clips that had been sprung loose and refastened in a new position.

All around the circular room now clips popped up and swiveled skyward. Then silence. Now Neary was aware of a different, sliding sound, continuous, slithery. His glance darted sideways, down, then up.

The ceiling was turning.

As Neary watched, the circular ceiling began to rotate in a counterclockwise direction. And, as it did, it seemed to get farther above Neary.

That was it, he told himself. The ceiling was unscrewing, like a bottle lid. It was rising. When he had first entered this room, it had been almost touching his head. Now it was ten feet above him and mounting rapidly.

Neary's face lifted skyward. The ceiling was twenty feet above him. Fifty. A hundred. Three hundred. New corridors appeared on the sides of the mother ship, new entrances to the center core as the ceiling lifted to reveal the entire vastness of the ship's interior.

Now it came to rest so far above Neary that he could barely make out its forms nearly a mile over his head. But, as it did, it also revealed how gigantic were the inner passages of this object from space.

From the roof of the mother ship's central core, far above Neary, hung a cluster of odd-shaped leaves or petals spread out in a circle like the leaves of an artichoke. They seemed to encase a busy, fiery core in which lights came and went.

Beyond these petals the roof of the mother ship was a vast display of flickering lights, not the stars of Neary's own sky but something more substantial. Waves of color seemed to wash across this immense sea of starlike points. Colors coalesced here and there, formed vague shapes, shifted, changed.

Neary blinked at the spectacle. It was a celestial picture show, an ever-changing display of forms and colors. Sometimes they looked familiar. Objects took shape that Neary could almost recognize. Then they faded, oozed into other forms, or disappeared completely.

Under the roof of the mother ship, encased by the gigantic petals, hung a kind of swarm of active, pulsating entities. They seemed to Neary, even from this distance, to be the UFOs with which he was now familiar, never at rest, shifting color, position, speed, shape. They vibrated to different rhythms as they shouldered in beside each other.

That was it, Neary realized. They were swarming like bees, clustering at the top of the mother ship's vast interior.

Now the petals began to close on them like down-dropping arms. It seemed to Neary that their destiny was to contain this hot, active core of UFO's, caging them into a commonality of energy and purpose.

Stray space fliers began zooming in through open

ports, hanging into the center swarm, and locking together with their neighbors. The whole panoply of UFOs pulsed and glowed in ripples of energy. A last ship hurried in through one port just as the petals clamped shut.

These ships, Neary saw, were individual units of the master force that powered this ultimate traveler in space, this ship-city that had come from another galaxy.

Their energy merged, melded, combined into a single irresistible force, Neary told himself. This was the secret of the ship's star-drive. This was the nature of its inhabitants, its social order, everything that had combined to bring it into Earth's orbit for this historic meeting.

Now the linkup was complete. A deep humming seemed to fill the cavernous reaches of the mother ship. Now a whirring of supernatural power overrode the bone-shaking hum. Neary could feel it through the floor, through his feet and legs. The light generated by the enclosed swarm of UFOs was rising to a pure white intensity that made his eyes hurt.

He was caught in an inferno of sound and light. He could feel a bright stab of fear across his shoulders. His heart was hammering inside his rib cage. Eyes narrowed to slits, he seemed locked in an upward stare, the great white-hot core of the UFO cage glowing hotter and hotter.

Beyond it, across the roof of the mother ship, starlike points flashed into colors and shapes. It seemed to Neary as if they coalesced for an instant into two forms.

Eyes. Two great eyelike shapes looked down at him. He no longer felt fear, only awe as he stared back into the endless depths of the almond-shaped eyes. Only understanding as the pure brilliance of the whiteness bathed and transformed him.

The light of knowledge, he thought. The light of truth.

I belong here, Neary thought.

Behind him the outer portal to the mother ship had closed. The immense space traveler was vibrating now. Technicians around the launching pad drew back from the increased light and heat.

Lacombe, Laughlin, and the others stood silently, watching.

And then, slowly at first, then faster, the great phantom starship began to lift off, easing away from its scaffold of light. The scaffold started to rise up around it. Soon it formed a brilliant, multicolored stairway up to the heavens, and the huge black ship, glowing at the edges now, rose up through layer after layer of clouds. Until this great city in the sky became the brightest of the brightest stars.

Jillian and Barry watched it all together. Jillian took one last picture of it all, the last of the most important pictures in the history of the world.

THE END

EPILOGUE

by Dr. J. Allen Hynek
Director, Center for UFO Studies

Thus we leave *Close Encounters of the Third Kind;* most of us with the feeling that the story we have just been told is just that—a story, but one which might come to pass. For where is the fine line between fantasy and that which is actually possible? Submarines, airships, and travel to the moon were once strictly out of Jules Verne. Yet, many of us observe the transition from fantasy to fact in our own lifetimes.

What then about Close Encounters of the Third Kind? Are these too only fantasies? Emphatically, no, if we can believe the many reports. In the book *The UFO Experience,* chapter ten was entitled "Close Encounters of the Third Kind." In it, there were many accounts of allegedly real experiences of just such encounters with occupants of UFOs. Such reports have come to me from many parts of the world. The events portrayed in the novel *Close Encounters of the Third Kind* were based in part on such actual reports. In particular, the appearance of the "extraterrestrials" in the novel were based on the most frequently re-

ported features of such beings. It will undoubtedly
surprise most readers to learn that there exists a cata-
log of some eleven hundred cases in which a UFO
occupant has been reported. This defines the term
Close Encounters of the *Third* Kind.

There are also Close Encounters of the First and
Second Kinds. The former is one in which a UFO is
seen very close up but no occupants are noted nor is
there any interaction with the immediate environment.
The latter, or Close Encounters of the Second Kind,
involve UFOs which leave some definite mark of their
presence. These can be burned patches of ground,
swirls of matted vegetation, broken tree branches, or
even evidence of radiation. The effects might be on
animals such as cows which refuse to give milk for
days after their UFO encounter. Or they might be on
purely inanimate matter such as moving vehicles
whose engines "conk out" in the presence of a brilliantly glowing object that passes over or close to
them. (Once the glowing object has departed, the
vehicle's engine is once again normally operable.)

These Close Encounters of the Second Kind are of
particular interest scientifically, for they enable us to
"bring the UFO" into the laboratory, so to speak, to
analyze the affected soil or plant samples, burned
leaves or branches. The Center for UFO Studies in
Evanston, Illinois, has many hundreds of each kind
of close encounter in its files. These bizarre and baf-
fling cases and the other kinds, too—the strange lights
seen at night, disc-shaped objects seen during the day,

and unexplained objects picked up on radar (and seen visually as well)—are being received, logged, and investigated by the Center for UFO Studies on an almost daily basis.

The UFO phenomenon is indeed real. Once the many false reports, based on misidentifications of normal objects or events, and the outright hoaxes have been sifted out, there remains a substantial and significant residue of unexplained reports that makes this subject truly worthy of serious scientific study; not just by the physical scientist but by the sociologist and the psychologist as well. The study of UFOs is indeed an interdisciplinary subject, and it is this approach that the Center has taken in its quest for the solution to the UFO problem. And if one asks why bother to solve the problem, the history of science has repeatedly given the answer: research in pure science has almost always led to the advancement and welfare of mankind. We never know where the quest for knowledge may lead.

If this book has stirred your imagination and curiosity and you should wish to learn more about current UFO sightings and particularly about the close encounters and what is being done about their study, we can do no better than to recommend the *International UFO Reporter*. The *Reporter* is a monthly newsletter which gives a round-up of the latest reported UFO cases and their analyses by qualified scientists and other experts who have studied and investigated actual UFO experiences.

The important work of the Center for UFO Studies is partly financed by subscriptions to the *International UFO Reporter*. In turn, the *Reporter* is the Center's major vehicle for keeping the public informed of progress toward the solution of the UFO phenomenon. The address for inquiries and subscriptions is *International UFO Reporter*, 924 Chicago Avenue, Evanston, Illinois 60202.